Drunk on Love
Twelve Stories to Savor Responsibly
Kerry Dean Feldman

Cirque Press
Copyright © 2019 Kerry Dean Feldman

All rights reserved. No part of this publication may be reproduced, distributed or transmitted in any form or by any means, including photocopying, recording, or other electronic or mechanical methods, without the prior written permission of the publisher, except in the case of brief quotations embodied in critical reviews and certain other noncommercial uses permitted by copyright law.

Published by

CIRQUE PRESS

Sandra Kleven — Michael Burwell
3978 Defiance Street
Anchorage, AK 99504

cirquepressaknw@gmail.com
www.cirquejournal.com

Book and Cover Design by Hal Gage
halgage.com

Cover Photo: *Anniversary Rose After 33 Years*, by Tami Phelps. Concept by Kerry Dean Feldman. Rose on cold wax painting, *Homage to Rebecca*.
www.tamiphelps.com

Cover and Author photo by Tami Phelps ©2019

Literary Fiction
ISBN 978-1-087-21978-3

Dedication

To:

Sandra Kleven, who suggested we do this;
Mike Burwell, who provided critical edits;
Don Stull of the U of Kansas who reads what I write and offers insightful critiques;
Tami Phelps, whose support for all I do is beyond words;
Koleen Parker, Mary Bouchoux, JoAnn Hertz—my sisters, who critique what I write; brothers Peter and Michael who are always with me in spirit;
Toni Lopopolo, my mentor who knows more about fiction than I knew was of concern; and her colleague, Shelly Lowenkopf, who suggested I move a sentence to begin the "Rules Of Thumb..." story, whose work, The Fiction Writer's Handbook, guided my understanding of the possibilities of fiction.

And,

Kathryn Marie Hauk-Feldman who taught me to read and write when I was five;
Sr. Mary Ruth, who told me, *WRITE*, long ago;
Sr. Mary Leonella, who taught me Shakespeare, and encouraged critical thinking;
Brie, my daughter, who always tells me, *DO IT*;
And Mayla Amell Elmore, exuberant grand-daughter age two, who might come to know me more than anyone.

Love will make men dare to die for their beloved—
love alone; women as well as men. (Phaedrus)

Plato, *The Symposium*

❧

Love...is the star to every wandering bark...

William Shakespeare, *Sonnet 116*

❧

Love...is a process, delicate, violent,
often terrifying to both persons involved,
a process of refining the truths they can tell each other.

Adrienne Rich, *On Lives, Secrets and Silence:
Selected Prose 1966–1978*

❧

Be drunk! So as not to be the martyred slaves of time,
be drunk, be continually drunk! On wine, on poetry
or on virtue, as you wish.

Baudelaire, *Les Fleurs du Mal*

Classical Greek Template Of Romantic Love

EROS
(the handsome God of erotic love)
pursues **PSYCHE**
(a lovely mortal princess with whom he falls in love)

Through Eros's love for Psyche,
and marrying her,
she becomes a goddess,
and,
as two gods,
live happily ever after on Mt. Olympus ...
(etc.)
(etc.)

Table of Contents

Rules of Thumb Among the Amazons 11

The Phaedra 21

Take My Yacht, Please 29

Of Moose and Men 39

Madisons of Bridges County 51

"Yesterday, Mom Had Blood" Poem 59

A Lover's Quarrel 61

Cosmic Conversation 69

Light Affairs 71

Cul-De-Sac 79

Deconstruction Among the Baobabs 87

"Daughter" Poem 101

When Winston Flats Came To Dundee 103

"Drunk on Love" Poem 129

It Happens In Instants 131

Drunk on Love
Twelve Stories to Savor Responsibly

Rules of Thumb Among the Amazons

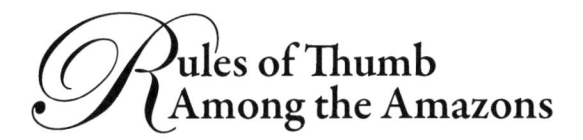

For instance, the common-law doctrine had been modified to allow the husband 'the right to whip his wife, provided that he used a switch no bigger than his thumb'—a rule of thumb, so to speak.

Del Martin, report on domestic violence in the U.S., 1976

I watched them while I waited for my hotdog. They raised their diplomas to San Francisco Bay, beyond Coit Tower, closed their eyes. They chanted like nuns, in unison, *Ommmmmmmmmmmm mani padme huuummmmmm.*

They looked at each other, held hands, screamed to the gates of The City below: FUUUUCKKK *YOUUUUU!*

Joy.

Three women who, prior to mid-life, completed bachelor's degrees in art, something I did but less appreciatively five years earlier. I completed my degree because you go to college at my age, graduate, but theirs was an adventure, a choice later in life. They'd scaled Everest, looped together, by the bonds of time and being women.

Wind from the bay billowed their dresses, Amazons ready to fly on any future's wind. This, a new truth in their lives, was about—them.

Another graduate, a younger woman, ran up, draped in a paper dress on which we scribbled our names and satirized art. She flung her arms around the three older women. A jazz band entertained us in the corner of the open-air square, Sonny Sharrock's restrained guitar frenzy, seizing rainbows.

I watched the women dance, laugh, unwind. I knew the blonde woman, Jenny, from my art criticism class. She waved to me; come join them. I never met the other two because I was shy around attractive women but also because of their age. Somewhere in their mid-thirties. I was twenty-seven, never fit in well with anyone who knew themselves well.

A script took shape in my mind, watching them, during their final year. A film for my graduate thesis, about how truth evolves. Three women, thirty-something in age, enter art school as undergraduates. My story; how completing the degree brought truth into their lives that had eluded them before.

How?

I would figure that out in Professor Jenkins' film thesis class in fall. The Prick—Jenkins.

One of the three friends, Kaerin, was married and sometimes brought her young son to class or met her husband at the water fountain after class. Her husband wore sports jackets with leather patches at the elbow, ill at ease with the inchoateness of the Art Institute. Kaerin was a rare student at the Institute: a happily married woman. Most of us worked out the angst of our young lives, real or imagined, through art. Rape, incest, parental abuse, hooked on heroin—The City wasn't all grassy parks and bridges and a place where you left your heart after a sweet summer love swoon.

The woman that intrigued me most, though, was the auburn-haired woman, Eve. She seemed an older Carol Alt, but weary around her eyes. She never spent time with anyone other than her two girlfriends. Her quietness suggested fragility, a trait I also had but which limited me. In her, the trait offered a guiding light, allowed her deeply, fearlessly, into darker regions within herself. There, in those dark regions, our instructors proclaimed, we should look for our inspiration. Where art lived. I saw it in her oil canvases—primordial blacks and reds colliding, sparks, the ache paint brings when you drip that fucking art-truth shit on...

'Scuse, me. I got carried away.

That's what I wished I could do in film.

Rashōmon, baby.

Kurosawa.

But I noticed a change in Eve during her final semester, as if she'd overcome whatever emotional burden brought her to art.

I responded to Jenny's urgent waving, joined the circle of Amazons, dancing.

Later, the graduated, almost-graduated, and a few instructors, went to Henry Hawaii's for the rest of the afternoon and into the night.

"A rule of thumb," Eve told me over her third margarita, "was the width of a stick a husband could use to discipline his wife, noted in early U.S. southern courts. Only as thick as your thumb, Arthur. Beyond that, illegal wife-beating. Thoughtful, weren't they?"

Eve smoked a cigarette, comfortably engaged in a mild form of, it seemed to me, flirting with and lecturing a younger man, obviously enchanted by her.

I pictured myself in a film. Evolving truth. Long shot—young man of average looks, clean-shaven, which is unusual for the times, sits at a table beside an attractive older woman. Close-angle—camera waist-high near him. He moves, puts his elbows on his knees, gazes hound-like at the woman. She wants him, too, he can tell.

Closeup of woman—her mind is elsewhere.

I went to the men's room, combed my hair, gave myself a talking-to, went back more internally distanced, mature.

"Arthur's coming off a love affair," Jenny kidded Eve across the table. "Be gentle."

The laughter which followed, once everyone checked to see I enjoyed the comment, felt good. Their laughter put my two months of confusion into perspective. Eve looked at me, did not join in the laughter, put her hand on my knee, out of sight of others. Silently consoled me.

The look, her touch, her unspoken concern—what was it?

I felt overwhelmed with the desire to have her know me. I sensed no need in her to challenge me to a male-female duel, or an endless negotiation about what we might not mean to each other. I summoned my courage before midnight, asked if she'd like to go with me to a bar where there was live music, a blues band.

She kindly refused, explained she would meet someone later. Her refusal, so delicately delivered—I felt only slightly embarrassed. The someone she met—my film instructor. They excused themselves. I wandered alone back to my flat.

I never liked Professor Jenkins, the ponytail, Lacoste cardigans or sweater draped around his neck. I refused to accept him as my guru. Without my bow at his shrine, he had little interest in my filmic work. The delight Eve evidenced in his presence, her renewed confidence in living, explained the change that came over her the past semester. Why had I not seen them together before?

When I woke the next morning, Eve's presence camped at the edge of my mind. Was the Samarai's Wife innocent? Seduced against her will, or was she willing?

A week later Jenny phoned, frantic.

"It's *Eve*. She's here and needs to talk. Kaerin's on duty at the hospital and I've got to run to the airport to pick up friends. Can you come over? *Right-fucking-away*, Arthur!"

Two buses later, I was at Jenny's apartment in the Castro District.

Jenny met me on her way out.

"It's Jenkins. He got engaged and never told Eve. She feels like an idiot, is hurt. Let her talk. See you all soon as I can. Don't let her leave alone. There's wine and cheese in the fridge. Thanks, Arthur."

Eve sat on the sofa, legs curled beneath her. She'd been crying but smiled when she saw me. Soon she cried again. I sat on the sofa, held her while she buried her face in the curve of my neck, calmed herself.

"Sorry," Eve said.

She got composed, touched her hair, poured us glasses of wine.

She suggested we talk in the back yard where the morning fog might bathe her mood. The grove behind Jenny's place offered peace.

"I don't care if he asked her to marry him, Arthur. I wasn't in love. But we'd been close, I thought, open and honest and vulnerable to each other. That's all I wanted, to share the experience with him. No reason to hide his engagement from me. He probably asked her before our last time together and what hurts was that was the best time with him. I wanted to remember that time and now he's made it meaningless. I knew he always wrote her, that she'd return someday, they might get married. I would have been glad for him. What fried me is they teach us to be open, to be vulnerable in our art, then he plays games with me. My husband was like that."

I didn't know Eve had been married. That explained her frayed look when I first saw her in art classes.

"How'd you learn about his proposal?"

"A friend. A woman who didn't know we were seeing each other. Hardly anyone knew about us."

I held Eve's hand.

"I never dated here, Arthur. Two years without a date after my marriage ended. Just bar-hopping with a gang, or a casual lunch. I came here from a

Seattle psycho ward—and months at home. I took pills after my divorce. I was careful here, getting my bearings. Jenkins seemed different. I trusted him. I want to call him now, tell him, *I forgive you*. I never wanted to be naive at thirty-five."

"I think Jenkins is in love with his image, Eve. He tries to be open but he's a technician. He knows what should happen in a film, how to reach an audience, but he can't do it himself. That's why he teaches instead of making films. Maybe remember the good times with him as all he was capable of?"

"I'm scared, Arthur," she said. "I'm starting to hate myself again. Walk me home, please? Jenny will need her place."

Eve and I walked through the Castro District, bought fresh fruit. I bought her a rose from a street vendor.

"Thanks. Why didn't Jenny introduce you before?"

"I'm shy."

She studied me. "Shy is not a disease, Arthur."

❦

Her apartment looked like my flat; a collage of art supplies, books, posters, dirty clothes and dirty dishes. Eve seemed more herself when she stuck bagels in the oven, cut up an apple, played the role of nurturer to a young man. I watched her, the amazing alternation a smile brought to her face, aligning muscles in a way that made her eyes larger, lips softer, more prominent. Some people look like wilted lettuce when they smile. But without a smile, Eve's face was a cardboard mask, flat, scarcely three-dimensional.

"Annie left me because I was sexually inadequate," I told Eve.

Pow, there it was. My truth.

Laid out like I couldn't ever admit to myself. "Let me be specific, Eve. This embarrassed me so much that when she left, I asked her not to tell her friends."

"About what?" Eve said.

"I could not perform the Gentleman's Courtesy for her."

I gave her knowledge of my own failure with someone I cared for. I had endless insecurities but found them defanged around Eve. Why Jenkins couldn't be open with Eve was his problem, not hers.

"The Gentleman's Courtesy? What is that? A twenty-something rite of passage?"

I became bolder.

"Pleasuring her with that which allows me to be loquacious and pronounce the letter, *L*. Okay?"

"Oh. That. None of my business. Seems ridiculous, though. Sex evolves between people. There shouldn't be little rules."

"No little rules of thumb?"

"Ah, yes. A good way to look at it. You in love with her?"

"Sort of, I think. I don't know."

A week later, Kaerin's marriage became rocky, a week Eve learned to put Jenkins out of her mind and I felt whole again.

Jenny and Eve knew of Kaerin's relationship with a student the past year but assumed it would quietly end when she received her degree and Kaerin moved on. But when Kaerin received her degree, she became unresponsive to her husband. That confused him because he thought she would be grateful for allowing her to go back to school. Kaerin told her husband about her romantic relationship, which at first her husband seemed to accept since he had a relationship also when her interests turned more to her art than to him.

Her husband wanted to know more about his adversary. Kaerin told him her lover and friend was a black man.

Her husband dissolved under the weight of the man's imagined prowess. He went nuts. Her husband seemed a confident sort of guy to me. A history professor at a local college. One night he slashed Kaerin's paintings in their garage, work to be part of her exhibition.

"Those aren't just paintings, they're me," she told him, in tears. "If you beat me, maybe I'd forgive you, but those are my soul you destroyed."

She moved into Jenny's apartment with her young son, Ricky.

Jenny asked if I could take them for a while at my flat because I had a spare bedroom.

Suddenly I had a woman and a child in my life, and a crazy husband who suspected me of being her new lover. Her son acted out his confusion by becoming ill, throwing up throughout the night, lying on a couch in front of the TV during the day. Kaerin continued her shifts as a nurse to support them through the mess and I became Ricky's babysitter.

Jenny and Eve helped me as much as they could. We five became a commune. Weekends we would picnic and sun at North Beach, take in the zoo, show Ricky the planetarium and pigeons at Union Square. Get a babysitter for Ricky on Saturday nights to allow us an evening out for a play or dinner.

Kaerin's husband began what seemed would become a long custody battle, but our companionship eased her depression and guilt.

One afternoon, after Ricky's father took him to a movie, neither of them returned. The following evening, Kaerin phoned the police. On the fourth day without her son, detectives came to my flat.

"You were sleeping with this other guy for how long?" a detective asked Kaerin.

Kaerin had been crying for days, the question broke her spirits.

I asked the detectives to come back later.

"Sorry, lady," the detective told her when he left. "If we're after a kidnapping-father, we have to know what it's about. To know his anger, how far he might take this. Understand? It's his kid, too, you know. Maybe you should have thought about..."

I told him to get the hell out.

"They'll find him, Kaerin," Eve told her. "You don't have to put up with that attitude by the police."

"He fought me every step of the way on my art degree," Kaerin said. "The house was a mess, meals never on time, not enough money for canvases and on and on. I needed an identity of my own is all, I told him. He couldn't see why. I wish to God I'd never needed one."

"Of course, you needed your identity. Don't feel guilty about that, ever," Jenny told her.

"I feel so dirty," Kaerin said through the tears, hair unwashed, face showing terror. "Malcolm's afraid to see me now, afraid he'll make things worse. He became the support I needed, a friend. That whole year we were only with each other a few times. We controlled how we felt for each other. I knew I was changing, experimenting, opening-up, but I wanted my husband to grow with me. He wouldn't or couldn't and I needed intimacy and trust and, Christ! I needed someone to believe in me. In me as me, not wife, mommy."

"These things happen," Eve said. "What evolved in you must have seemed an overnight flip to your husband. Men don't see why they're not enough. Why a woman wants her identity, outside of wife and mother. They haven't been prepared."

"I tried to tell him," Kaerin said. "It made less and less sense to him. I gave up trying to explain. Maybe I stopped respecting him, is that what happened? I loved him but couldn't respect him? Malcolm never pushed anything between us beyond a friendship, that part of it was me. I needed him, wanted him, wanted to feel SOMETHING. He had his battles to fight, too, and I tore up his image of himself as a black-power rebel. He feared wanting to make love with me made him a cliché, desiring my white skin. Finally, he saw me as a woman and skin-color made no difference."

She was working it out in her mind in our presence.

When I watched them chant their mantra at the graduation, part of my envy had been for their camaraderie as they reigned over the city. I thought they had some sort of mystical women openness. But their deepest self-judgments had not been shared, or, perhaps, their evaluations of each other's decisions. Perhaps their friendship would have collapsed if any judgment had been rendered, and without it each woman could not, alone, take on the world and its expectations of women.

My *Rashōmon* film about them dissolved. I'd never understand such complexity.

My film was now about me.

My ex-girlfriend, Annie, looked surprised to find three attractive women in my apartment. I was surprised to find Annie at my door.

"Hadn't heard from you. I missed you," she said. "Who are these people?"

"Friends. I'll explain later," I said.

"Just wanted to talk, have lunch. Are you living with one of them?"

"No. I'll explain. Sure, lunch is fine. I'll introduce you and we can leave. My place is more theirs than mine now anyway."

Eve gave me a supportive look when Annie and I left, a supportive but cautionary Amazon look. I smiled, gave Eve a thumbs-up exit.

That night we ended up at Annie's for dinner. Fettucini with Alfredo sauce. The extent, I knew, of Annie's culinary expertise, and I appreciated her willingness to cook for us. Annie lived on frozen dinners, creamed cheese, raisin bagels and apple juice.

After dinner, she suggested we make love.

I put intimacy with Annie as far from my mind as I could for two months. Without much ado, we went to bed.

And there it was—the mystery. Annie hot and moaning, the fettucine working in me. Her legs wide, she lifted her bounty for my errant tongue. I performed the Gentleman's Courtesy for her very well, best I could tell from the unusual sounds she made. Almost a song.

Which led to questioning, much later, as to the source of my newly discovered lack of inhibition.

"Just discussing it with that woman, Eve, dissolved your problem?"

"When I tried it before on you, Annie, I saw a baby's head ready to emerge. That vision has vanished."

"You didn't practice with Eve?"

There seemed a taste of jealousy in her words. A sweet taste, to me.

"Does it matter?"

"I'd just like to know, for Christ's sake. I mean, a miracle, like water-walking. Awesome, Arthur."

"I told you. We just talked."

"I can't believe it. You acquired consummate skill. That takes practice."

"I'm not a machine. Don't wreck it for me, okay, Annie?"

I sensed, as I took the bus home, that my caring for Annie sloughed from me sometime during my excellent performance and riding that bus, me alone on the planet with my evolving truth, except for my commune. Amazons or Sirens?

At home, I found Kaerin asleep on the couch, Eve finishing a week's dishes, waiting up should I return that night.

"You okay?" Eve said, her hair rolled in a bun, frayed strands backlit by the bare bulb above the sink, her jeans stained with soap and pizza below an Institute sweatshirt.

"Yes. No. I don't know. Is Kaerin alright?"

"She's fine. Police called. They found her son and husband at her husband's sister's home."

"Ricky?"

"Doesn't seem to know anything weird happened. Just an outing with his father. Kaerin will have Ricky back tomorrow."

"Good. I'll walk you home," I said.

"I can take a cab, Arthur. You need space now, I think. You look wiped."

"I want to walk you home," I said. "It's late. The dark time when crazies roam."

"Okay, thanks. But it's a long hike," Eve said. "And if we're attacked, Arthur, let me handle it."

At Eve's apartment I cried, quietly. I don't know why. She didn't ask for a reason, made us tea, put on music, Shaka Khan singing one of my favorites, "Ain't Nobody."

...I want this night to last forever...

Eve stands above me, arms folded across her chest, her hip juts to the side as the other takes her weight. Amazon woman. She takes my cup, places the cup on the coffee table, guides me to my feet.

We hold each other, dance slowly, our cheeks gently touching.

"I'm going to Chicago for graduate school," Eve said, "although I'll have to stay here till January because I missed their fall deadline. They liked my work. They really liked my work, Arthur. I heard from the department chair today. I'll have a full scholarship."

"I'm happy for you. May I visit you? Chicago?"

"I haven't left, yet. We can be with each other, all you want. Beginning tonight."

We undressed, held each other in her bed.

Her lips softer, warmer, more informative, than any woman's I ever tasted.

When I performed the Gentleman's Courtesy on Eve, I felt like Adam must have felt, in the Garden, but so perfect I would never know a Garden like that again.

Eve moved down, said, "Arthur, I want you to know a woman's welcome. Lay back. There's nothing, now, for you to do. I will take you to that place on my canvas where black and red collide. Never been there myself, yet."

"*What?*"

"I said not *yet*, Arthur."

I never made my *Rashōmon* film. Switched schools. I got to know the winds that blow off Lake Michigan and how much I needed to grow the fuck up.

Eve told me, later, "Her name is *Chaka* Khan, Arthur."

The Phaedra

or

A Socratic Dialogue on Man and Woman in Make-Believe Costume Rental, Inc., Pico Boulevard, Santa Monica

> *Love is a serious mental disease.*
> Plato, *Phaedrus*

Phaedra rested in the corner of Make-Believe, Inc., watching me wait on customers needing costumes for Halloween. A mother dressed in a Katherine Hamnet, wrinkled-chic-khaki blouse, with leather pants, searched through the gloves box.

"She wants *Gone with the Wind* gloves," she said, in reference to her daughter's request. "Scarlett O'Hara gloves, mom."

The woman's back faced me, then she bent over, her butt facing me as if I was one of the mannequins I rented. I let her rummage through the cardboard box—we weren't formal here.

Phaedra, I noticed, had her quaint, almost mystical smile in place, her blonde wig slightly awry. Mothers amused her. Phaedra had no womb.

Across from Phaedra in the loft overlooking the shop rested Socrates. He, his bust, surrounded by Civil War costumes. The Civil War costumes were rarely rented. I marveled at the changing fantasies of Santa Monica. Men somehow knew that southern chivalry was dead, that women no longer believed much in such fantasy, especially in any chivalry associated with war. *Rambo* killed the belief. *Star Wars* resurrected the myth, but in Outer Space, in "a land far away." Vietnam made war on earth smell foul. Or clarified its purpose. War was meant for killing, not for chivalry. The "gooks" taught us something about ourselves— our own savagery. Reagan tried to make war chivalrous with marines invading places reminiscent of the tiny country in *The Mouse That Roared*, where warriors had only spears to hurl when Manhattan was invaded. Then Iraq. Socrates, of course, had known this about war for over two thousand years. Perhaps he had seen it in crazed Spartan eyes. Phaedra had known it, sensed it, for as long as Woman existed. The daughter of the khaki-bloused lady would learn it soon enough. War between nations, war between the sexes—chivalry was dead.

Socrates told me once, in reference to war, "Men are slow learners about life because they feel they can control life."

Phaedra tossed him a condescending smile at that remark, as if to say, "You got credited by history for having a lot of brains by discovering things as obvious as *that*?"

The khaki-bloused lady waved long white gloves at me in triumph. I wrote up the charges, watched her hurry out, another parental task accomplished in another day she did not own.

"Ahhh, Mothers. You know, no one ever asked what my mother was like," Socrates said.

He mostly talked to himself. Socrates never spoke when customers were in the store, as I asked him not to. He scared me quite thoroughly one night when, as I was looking for a Darth Vader helmet to complete an inventory check, he said, "You know, it's true. Willy Nelson's beard looks like a woman's hairy mound."

I had never heard Socrates speak before that.

Phaedra, whom I named years earlier when some friends and I created her from the bottom half of a wire sewing dummy and a department store torso, with a beautiful face we found at a garage sale, coughed a laugh at his remark. Anything can happen near or around tinsel-town, I realized, as my friendship with the two of them began—once my arteries flowed again with blood.

They chatted after hours for many years, just to each other, but it was news to me.

Usually they just debated. The war of the sexes in my loft.

Socrates had two thousand years over Phaedra, plus a good rep behind him. But she had a woman's intuition which allowed her, she said, "To cut through the crap."

Socrates told her, "You'd think differently about a lot of things if you'd ever been laid."

His Greek chauvinism had never been much challenged—women in Athens couldn't even vote, or file for a divorce unless they escaped from their homes and beat a husband's slave to the court. Usually, though, some guy tipped off the husband that his wife was hell-bent for the judge, a slave would be sent to grab her and that was that.

But Phaedra had known no other world except the modern world, which began for her in my garage during the year Geraldine Ferraro was a Vice-Presidential running-mate to whatshisname. Hers was a world of Margaret Thatcher, *Ms.* magazine, birth-control pills (which she knew about but had no need for), and ERA rallies, reported regularly on the TV I kept running for company. Phaedra assumed equality with men, and maybe felt a little superior to Socrates who was only a bust. I felt no need to protect her from his verbal jousting. While I added up receipts for a day or repaired buttons on cloth, they bantered, letting me join in sometimes, but usually finding me too civil to move the discussion on much.

Socrates once said to me, in disgust, "You can't kill mom in your brain, can you, Alan? She lives there in your cranium as some Big-Breasted-Spider Woman-Cum-Sister-To-Adore-You."

Socrates believed in overkill, obviously.

That night Phaedra said to him, "Ok, Socrates, let's hear about your mommy. What was the mother of a great Greek philosopher really like? Did she *love* you?"

"So," Socrates smiled, as he drawled like a Greek Willy Nelson, "What is love, sweetheart?"

Another dialogue had begun.

Phaedra responded as if her button had been pushed, "Love is the assumption that one or more persons on the planet are more special than all the rest."

Socrates stared at her, astonished, telling her, "By Jove, I've never heard it broken down to one sentence so deftly. That's brilliant. Plato spent years and years rambling on and on about love, as was his wont, making this qualification, that qualification. You, however..."

Phaedra broke in, "I, dear Socrates, am incapable of loving anyone, so I see it more clearly. Perhaps. Truth, you see, *is an evolving complexity.*"

"No!" Socrates shot back. "No, damnit! Truth, real Truth, just IS. Now and forever unchanging."

"*Bullshit,*" Phaedra said.

"Phaedra, dear," Socrates said, calmly, "because you think you cannot love you assume that you can be objective about love, but if you could love, you assume you'd think differently."

"Give me a womb, then I'd love," she said.

Then she grew silent, stared absently at the wall.

"Women don't love with their wombs, for God's sake. But with their *minds*, as *all people do*," Socrates said.

Phaedra looked at him with a pitying glance. "You are not a woman. You don't know. If you had a womb, your *brain* would think differently, old man, old friend."

"Look," he said "I don't have a phallus, a prick. Yet, I can still love, love with my mind, my higher faculties."

Phaedra smiled. The old man's admission of genital vulnerability touched her.

"Maybe," she said, "that is one reason why we can be good friends. Having the organs we lack seems to lead to more problems than they solve between men and women. Communication blocks."

But Socrates had begun humming. He'd already left the question regarding proper anatomical plumbing. He hummed to himself when he was on new turf.

I took the lull as a time to ask Phaedra if she wanted her wig removed for a while, her skull scratched. She said that would be nice. I put away the clown costume I was sewing a button on, went to the back of the store to the ladder rungs nailed to the wall, climbed up. I removed her Marilyn Monroe wig, began the massage she enjoyed.

"*Mmmmm*," she said, her eyes closed. "I like how you touch me. Wish I had arms. You touch so well, Alan. So giving, so sharing."

Socrates piped in, "My mother wanted me to be an Archon, hold an office like Solon. Solon's mom was very proud of him."

We looked at him. Socrates was back to his mom.

"My mom said, 'I'm not allowed to vote, Soccy, so you must become a politician. I made you a member of the upper crust, my womb and your father's money as a sculptor. I'll vote through you, have my rights through my son.'"

He seemed pensive, sad, remembering some lost view of his life someone else had had for his life.

"My mother was tougher then I," he said. "She should have been Archon. I could only philosophize."

Phaedra said, "Tougher?"

"She seemed to lack all concern about justice. Yet, somehow, she taught me to believe in a rational world. She just did 'what worked', she said, a pragmatist. Xerxes would never have stood a chance against her. *I sure as hell didn't.*

Phaedra stopped my rubbing. "Dear," she said to me, "would you rub my bosom? Beneath this *goddawful* robe you stuck on me."

I put the wig back on her, gave the wig a few fluffs. I rubbed her bosom.

She had no arms, a quiet Venus de Milo. Her breasts were firm, coming to dramatic painted strawberry tips, pointed upward as if her male creator did not comprehend gravity and breasts in his mannequin fantasies.

"*Oooo*, that feels so good, Alan," she said. "I can almost feel it between my legs, but I have no legs. No *Mons Venus*."

She cried, quietly.

Then she cried out, "*I'm missing the drama of my gender.* Damn! Damn you, Alan, for making me half a woman. Damn you, Socrates, for being content to enjoy only my mind."

I felt like hell.

Socrates, unperturbed by her outburst, said, "Alan saved you from the threat of rape, my dear. Be grateful."

"Ohhhh, go mentally masturbate, you old synapse," she screamed.

"I do think you somehow managed to have menstruation, dear Phaedra," Socrates said. "You sound as though it's that time of the month."

Socrates could be cruel with his logic. I recalled my own arguments with my ex-wife, my insensitivity to her emotional complexity, to many simple expressions of vulnerability on her part. She was an actress. I told Socrates to shut up. I put my arms around Phaedra, hugged her.

She whispered, "*Make love to me.*"

"What?"

"Let's make love, have sex. Turn Socrates to the wall and make love to me, whisper things in my ear of passion and beauty, let me feel your maleness, your desire for me, touch all of me there is to touch. I'll do things for you no woman has ever done. I love you."

This was nuts. Yet, I felt aroused. Nature had such simple, crazy plans for us. For gender.

"I can't, Phaedra," I said. "Wouldn't be right. We're friends. It would confuse everything. And I don't know how to, exactly."

I checked to see if Socrates could hear us. He seemed lost in thought.

The truth was: that at that moment, I desired her. Something had happened, a closeness. But I knew I couldn't, shouldn't. Phaedra was not real, not fully. I was a human, she wasn't. I treasured her company: I loved her mind not her body, her half an upper body, her armless body with the bald head.

Then I thought of my ex-wife, Ellen, who had lain beside me, naked, night after night, as if she was a mannequin. I had loved Ellen. But she had loved... what? Phantasms. In her mind. Men whose strangeness to her allowed her to feel safe and unknown, perhaps. How complex our simplicity, we rational animals. I felt an urge to undo with Phaedra what I failed with in Ellen. The pain I carried long enough. I kissed Phaedra, lovingly, on her painted lips. Her lips felt alive with love and caring and need. Wet with salty tears she shed. Her lips seemed free, bound only by need. I had been stuck in that shop, too, day after day, making a living.

Who was free?

The first time in written history the word "freedom" had been used was by some Sumerian King four thousand years ago, a man who controlled slaves, who fought wars, whose descendants watched the end of humankind's first civilization.

"O, for God's sake," Socrates groaned, aware of our embrace.

I went to him, turned him to the wall, facing a confederate flag, Rhett Butler's flag, chivalry's flag, the flag of evolving truth.

Somehow Phaedra and I made love, breaking rules, making new ones. Living out her evolving truth. I realized I had been living many lies. A kind of Kundalini realization that I was, had been, as unreal as the place where I worked, as the make-believe world just north in L.A. where Hollywood evolved. I realized that I hated what I did, selling costumes, preparing others for fantasies.

I wanted to write, to write my guts out no matter who read the shit I wrote. I realized I hated Ellen and that the feeling was okay and that my anger was okay, and that Ellen was okay. I realized I had lived in fantasy as a child much too long, that somehow it hadn't ended, that my adult world was a continuation of the cowboys and Indians games, of my Schwinn bike which to me had been Champion, Gene Autrey's movie horse, of sports contests in which football games I won seemed to live in me as bigger harvests of myself rather than fantasy combat.

I hugged the peaceful Phaedra, put a shawl around her shoulders, went to the ladder.

"Socrates was right," Phaedra said. "A bit, anyway, about what I needed. I felt fire and wind in me, the passion of the ages and it-all-seems-different now. I won't ask again, Alan. *Peace, my love.*"

"Peace, Phaedra," I said.

"And did we practice safe sex, Phaedra?" Socrates said, giggling, his nose close to the confederate flag.

I turned out the lights in the shop, locked the door.

The night air was cool. I headed for the Santa Monica beach, trying to grasp what everything I realized would mean to my life.

It meant doing this, on this beach, with a roller-skater going by behind me on the concrete.

Writing the truth, for the first time in my life, which, of course, no one would believe.

Take My Yacht, Please

I watched the little blue tetras chase each other in the aquarium. The receptionist finally said he'd see me. At a hundred and fifty an hour, I hope so, I wanted to tell her.

Instead, I said the tetras looked overfed. She said Doctor Morris fed the fish; none died of overfeeding.

Why did I need to antagonize everyone?

I headed up the carpeted stairs. Even the calm of the waiting area annoyed me. I hated to show up at *Neptune's*, hated the Pico reed on my lip, the sound of blues coming from my sax. When you're too blue for the blues, you're fucked. The blonde I'd gotten involved with fried my brain. I knew why. I feared she'd show up at *Neptune's Dive*, perfumed and gorgeous. And afraid she wouldn't.

My hand about to grab the doorknob, Doc Morris stepped out of his office like a jack-in-the-box. Like the clown that popped out of the hand-cranked tin box my folks gave me when I was three, which I lost when we buried my mom and moved. It unnerved me to have the Doc pop out of his office like that, no cranking on my part allowed. I glanced around, any surveillance cameras? Like those in a 7-11 with a sari-wrapped woman behind the counter, a red dot between her eyes? Third eyes everywhere these days. No one trusting anybody.

At the end of the hall, in the corner of the ceiling, I spotted a camera. So, Doc Morris is a control freak, wants to know if some nut comes gunning for him. Now I knew more about him than he did about me.

He's my height, tanned, balding, graying around his dome like the old gulls that dropped bird shit on my boat house. I wanted in his office fast, so no one would see me, think I was crazy.

"I'm Doctor Morris," he says, shaking my hand once, then letting go like he feared I might think he was gay. Or maybe he thinks I'm gay? Shrinks aren't afraid of things like that, are they? They've been analyzed and aren't nut cases themselves.

"Willy," I say.

Somehow this means we now know each other. I'm supposed to spill my guts to a stranger. I look around his office to get a feel for the guy. He motions to a stuffed chair, sits across from me in a swivel chair, in front of his oak desk. There's an aquarium behind him and a huge photograph of a sailboat, a yacht, above the fish tank. A large Macintosh screen on his desk. I wonder what Freud's office looked like. No pictures of Doc Morris's kids or wife. His office furniture is egg white, like almost everything in the room. The guy has bucks. I calculated in the waiting area that shrinks could earn a thousand a day at his rate and only have to see six nut cases a day, five days a week.

Twenty grand a month.

I could own my own nightclub with dough like that.

"How can I help you, Willy?"

Felt like I was going to confession. I'd confess my sins, get a rosary for penance. If they still did confessions. My mom always took me to confession. After her death, I stopped going.

"I'm seeing a woman, a married lady, little older than me, and she won't let me go."

Might as well get it out. Hide nothing. I'd been banging some rich old guy's wife. I wanted to set the story for him, explain I never knew she was married. That I was innocent. At first, anyway. The Doc lived here, knew that bored ladies filled Newport Beach, married to rich old guys who never spent much time with them. Maybe something like Doc Morris's yacht. Take her out for a cruise now and then, feel good knowing she's secured at the marina, waiting to be boarded when he had time. Accessorize the hell out of her. Like the kept-ladies who hadn't heard that the life they were drawn to had ended. I avoided married women. My ethics and sense of self-preservation.

"Willy," he tells me, "I'm a psychiatrist, not a counselor. I work with people who have emotional disorders, brain dysfunctions, traumatic experiences." He says he doubts I need him, at his price, for my "situation." Though he's sure it's troubling me a lot. A gentle let-down.

"I can't sleep or eat, Doc. My brain's down," I plead. "If she makes a scene, brings in her husband, gets me fired where I play music...."

He shows some interest. "You play *music*?"

We talk and I learn he likes Big Mama Thornton, Eddy Cleanhead Vinson, Lloyd Glen. He never gets out to clubs, too busy. Those folks he knew about were blues players few white guys ever heard of. I'm impressed. He even knew Gatemouth Brown. Every wanna-be cool white guy in America heard of Miles Davis, or Muddy Waters. Doc Morris wins me over when he talks about Big Boy Crudup. All this interesting chitchat cost me twenty bucks. I took the conversation back to me.

"She came in a few months ago to listen to music, she said. Bought me a drink, waited till our set ended for the night. Gorgeous. Not pushy. Sophisticated. An older lady but in great shape. Like the lady in *Someone To Watch Over Me*. You see that movie? Well, like that lady. Velvet voice."

Morris tries to sit still. His plump fingers playing rub-a-dub on his knee. I guess he wants a paranoid schizophrenic to work on. I'm asking a Jaguar engineer to fix a Yugo. He needs someone to write a prescription for, take a pill, not jump off a building. I read in *Rolling Stone* that shrinks don't talk to clients about wanting to screw their mothers anymore. No, they say your brain is like a Honda factory with a bunch of robotic parts, only it's a gland. Like a pancreas or something. All I knew was my brain ached. No pill would solve a neuro-receptor problem in my gland. Maybe, I thought as I had read that article, shrinks missed something. Something they'd blocked out about their own mothers.

I said, "She reminds me of my mother."

His fingers stopped drumming. Maybe I hit something from his graduate student days long ago, some ancient Freudian lecture the medical establishment now told him was garbage. It's easier to collect insurance payments if you prescribe pills for neuro-receptors. I only knew I was fucked up, my vision starting to blur. When fantastic sex is part of what's making you feel bad, you're fucked up.

"Your mother?" he said.

"She was sophisticated, too," I tell him. "And bored. She loved to hear me practice my sax as a kid, though. I didn't bore her. But, Doc, my mother drowned herself when I was fourteen."

Well, there it was. I never talked about that to anyone.

I tried to concentrate on what Morris said, but behind him, in his fish tank, I saw a beta floating on top of the water. Must have died sometime between when I entered and now. I said, "There's a dead fish in your tank."

He turned to the tank. No concern showing like I thought there should be. His tanned face, expressionless as a suede jacket. He went to the tank, lifted the lid. "You're right. Guess I overfed her, or she got the Ick."

He scooped the beta with a net, wrapped her in a blue tissue from a Kleenex box next to the tank. Dropped her in a wastepaper basket under his desk. "Sorry for the interruption," he said.

I now feel uncomfortable with him. I thought of my dad's indifference when they found my mother's body on the beach. Death made me sad; any dying made me sad. I try never to see death.

"Sorry," he said again, returning to the chair across from me. "When you were fourteen...?"

I told him I didn't want to talk about when I was fourteen. I wanted to talk about me now, at thirty-three, and Helen.

"Helen?"

That was the name she gave me, I told him, but maybe it's not her real name. She didn't want me to know anything real about her. Keep it fantasy, for good sex. She was forty, I learned by accident. She wanted no way for me to call her, track her down outside *Neptune's Dive* and my bed, do something crazy like call her at her home and get her husband, mess up her life. She only wanted to be my *Helen-Of-Troy*, she said. Feel my music between her legs, fuck my brains out. That's how she put it, too. And that's what she did. She liked to talk dirty and talk about art and her feelings and listen to me play, just for her.

She needed more, she said. More *what*? *Space*, she said. Once, crying, she said, "More of me, Will."

Morris said the obvious. Why didn't I call her bluff about making trouble and stop seeing her? I saw his point. Maybe I overfed her.

"I love her, Doc," I confessed.

The old snake. Love. Font of all the blues. I avoided it till now, never wanting to love anyone again, I told him.

"*Again?*"

"After, you know, my mom."

And in that answer, I cleared up a mystery about myself. I realized I never wanted to be close to any woman again. Or anyone. I felt closer to this Morris guy in the thirty minutes we'd eaten up than to anyone I knew. But I realized it wasn't because I hated my mother for killing herself. It was because I never wanted to feel such a loss again. A rejection I never understood.

"I hate my mother," I said. "And *I love her.*"

I felt tears come.

Morris said, "So, you weren't looking for love with this ... *Helen?*"

No, I tell him, feeling a panic. My words tumbled out, like notes from Cleanhead Vinson's cut about being chased by some lady's husband. My words bumping into each other.

"...and she never told me she was married at first...just lonely...and me, too... would I play for her alone some time...marvelous body and so warm and sexy... dreams of her at night...so elegant...I didn't deserve her...a moonlight swim and making love to her in the water, and then we became friends, laughing...and my music got smoother and raunchy and she told me she was married when I asked her to move in, after she hooked me on her body and kindness and she knew I needed her...and she said she couldn't leave him, not now, and why?...because I'm not ready to, she said, he's too old and boring...never talked to her but she liked his money and O, god, could she make love...then one day she said maybe she loved me and I learned her blond hair was a wig and that she needed money to feel safe and he owned a yacht and she loved Cancun vacations *and she'd wreck my life if I tried to leave her because now she needed me to make her life perfect....*"

I broke down, spilled it all to Morris. His face changed, blood left his fat cheeks. He turned turnip red, beginning at his neck, moving up his face. Like maybe he's having a heart attack.

"You *okay?*" I said.

He took a breath, nodded he was okay. I stood, got a tissue from the Kleenex box next to his fish tank to blow my nose, wipe my eyes.

He said, quite perturbed, "*CANCUN?*"

"Doc, stop repeating everything I say like we're playing some free association game."

I blew my nose, felt sorry about my outburst. He only tried to help me, after all. "I'm sorry," I said.

I felt my head about to explode and now I was attacking him for no reason. Get a grip, Willy. I glanced at the photograph of his yacht above the fish tank.

"Nice boat," I said, calmer, sitting down.

"Yeah, thanks."

He became quiet. When, finally, he spoke, I heard lead in his voice.

"Mr. Blake," (I noticed the formality as he read from my intake form), "we seem trapped in our fish tank, don't we?"

I said, "Well, yeah, maybe, if you want to get philosophical."

The image of Dustin Hoffman through a fish tank came to mind, with the keys at the bottom thrown by Mrs. Robinson. Morris was a very smart guy.

"You and me, we're like Neptune, at the bottom of the sea," he said.

I told him I played at *Neptune's*, is all I knew about myth stuff.

"You don't get it, do you, Mr. Blake. Willy?"

"Get *what*?"

"Well, I do," he tells me, drums his fat fingers on his desk. "I am King Neptune and my kingdom is *mine*."

"Great. But you're not making any sense, Doc."

"I can't be your psychiatrist, Willy."

"Why?"

"Oh, professional ethics, let's say."

I pleaded, telling him he's cleared up a huge problem, about my mother and fearing love and we're only half way through the session.

"Just the tip of the iceberg, Will," he says.

"You think I'm nuts, Doc? That I need pills?"

"No," he says, "I think you need *to get the hell out of town*, if you know what's good for you."

I said that sounded more like Clint Eastwood than a psychiatrist.

Maybe it was, he went on. But he'd talk to me straight now, *like a friend*. Some problems were just too... (he searched for a word) ... *Big* to handle, he tells me. I could move to L.A. where studio bands pay a lot more than what I earned at *Neptune's*, he goes on. Or to San Francisco. Or to Chicago. I noticed the cities were farther and farther from Newport Beach.

"*Or to Bumfuck Egypt!*" I tell him, getting pissed off.

Running away wouldn't solve anything. I'd just take my problem with me, between my ears. And, besides, I was broke, I told him. I leaned forward, elbows on my knees, rubbing my hands together like a neurotic, trapped, housewife.

Love makes you nuts.

Maybe my mother discovered that, too.

Then Morris stunned me. "Maybe I could help out on that. Say, five thousand?"

"Five grand? You'd give me *five grand* so I'd leave, get started somewhere else?"

Psychiatrists were more concerned about a patient than in any Woody Allen movie.

"Or ten," he said, squeezed his knuckles, popped his knuckles too loud for my taste.

"No," I said, irritated. "I solve my own problems."

"Willy," he said, "some problems are beyond us. We have to let go."

Then he sounded threatening. "Sometimes our problems sink us. *Kill us*."

I pulled out a Winston though there was a No Smoking, Please sign on the wall. I lit up. He said smoking wasn't allowed in his office. I put it out on the bottom of my shoe. Without thinking I lit another one. He said nothing, bummed a Winston from me, tore off the filtered end. He pulled a lighter from his desk drawer and an expensive blown-glass ashtray. He blew smoke rings.

"What do you *want*, Willy? Really, really want?" he said. "You want to get laid, the best fucking you ever had. Or, to live well, at least stay alive?"

"I don't know, for Christ's sake. That's why I'm here. All you're doing is confusing me."

"Trust me. You've got to trust somebody, right? If not your psychiatrist, then who? Twenty. My last offer. Take it or leave it. If you know what's good for you... and Helen... you'll take it."

The cigarette helped me think. Maybe he could write it off on his taxes. But I couldn't take his boat. On the other hand, maybe he tried to get my unconscious kicked into gear like he did with the question about why I couldn't love again.

I decided to go along, what with a hundred and fifty bucks an hour I shelled out.

"Well, Doc, if you're trying to get me to consider an offer I can't refuse, to leave Newport..."

"Yes, Blake. That's what I want you to consider. *For your mental health*."

"If I was to leave..." I thought real hard, trying to heal myself, "Well," I said, "It'd be nice to have," my eyes shot behind him to the photograph, "a yacht."

I laughed, feeling a bit loony.

He blinked once, hard, squashed his Winston in the ash tray, walked to the photograph of his lovely yacht lifted the framed picture off the nail, brought the photograph to me.

"I'll sign the transfer papers on her tomorrow and throw in five thousand. Take her, please. I never got to ride her as much as I wanted but I loved her. I really did. Just got too busy. Have a good life, Willy, someplace else. And, *your fifty minutes are up.*"

Morris had tears in his eyes. I put an arm around him, took the photograph in a daze. In pencil, at the bottom of the matte around the photograph, I read, "*Helen-Of-Troy, Cancun.*"

Morris ushered me out of his office, telling me to meet him tomorrow at his bank and not tell Helen what was up so she couldn't foul it up.

I didn't know what to say. I said, "You feed your fish too much, Morris."

He said, "Yeah, I'll have to work on that."

He shut the door.

I heard him stumble against his swivel chair or kick it. Anyway, he swore like hell. I wondered who *his* shrink was.

Next day I met him at his bank, not knowing if this was part of an acting-out therapy technique or what. He got the boat ownership papers from his safety deposit box, signed the boat over to me.

Morris seemed like the dad I never had, so I wanted him to see Helen's picture. As the paper sign-over was being notarized, I took a photo of Helen from my wallet to show to Morris. I confessed that I couldn't keep all this from Helen. That she decided when I told her maybe it was for real that I was getting a yacht that she would leave her husband. She said she would sail around the world with me, till the money ran out. See if we really liked each other.

Morris' face lost color.

Maybe I destroyed his therapy plan for me?

"That's *not* the deal we made, Blake!" he yelled, grabbed the picture of my Helen.

His mouth sagged, looking at my Helen, like a dog's mouth when sprawled in hot sun. "*That's not Helen.*"

I assured him it was Helen, without her wig. I wondered what he thought she was supposed to look like. Prettier? Older? I didn't know what upset him so.

"In fact," I told him, "she's on her way to meet us. Wants to thank you for helping us. She thinks you're one unbelievable guy."

I saw Helen in the bank lobby. She wore jeans, a heavenly tight T-shirt and didn't look forty. I ran to her, hugged her, handed her the deed to the boat.

Helen tucked it in her purse.

Morris looked devastated.

"I thought..." Morris said. God only knows what Morris thought.

Helen hugged Morris, thanked him for helping her realize she had to live honestly, that love was more important to her than anything else. That taking a risk, as Morris did by giving his yacht to me, was what life was about.

Risking it all, for love.

Helen divorced her husband without asking for an arm and a leg. He'd been getting a little on the side himself, it turned out. Helen (which was her real name after all) and I sailed around the world.

When we got back to Newport, I sold Morris' yacht, used the money as a down payment on *Neptune's Dive*.

One night, Doc Morris showed up with his wife at our club. He looked ten years younger. After introducing me to his lovely wife, also named Helen, he thanked me for helping him learn more about himself in fifty minutes and one yacht than he'd learned in six years of analysis.

Well, what's a buddy for? He and his wife held hands, cooed like lovebirds.

The four of us sail in Morris' new sailboat. My Helen manages our club as half-owner and we got married. I send my musician friends to Morris for therapy. Male bonding, I tell my buddies, nothing like it.

Of Moose and Men

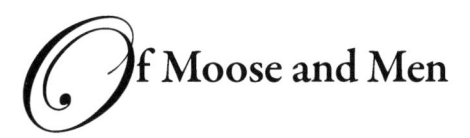

> *The best laid schemes o' mice an' men*
> *Gang aft a-gley,*
> *An' lea'e us nought but grief an' pain,*
> *For promised joy!*
>
> Robert Burns, "To A Mouse"

The Harley breathed easier, so did Nate, the further north he rode. From Tuskegee up Highway 65 to Birmingham, on to Nashville where he rode the ribbon of Highway 24 into Kentucky.

Somewhere near Eddyville, he lost the Faith. With that sloughing from him like the old skin of snake, Nate hoped his addictions to easy truth, easy love, and Fundamentalist security, fled in the wind behind him.

Crossing the Tennessee River near Paducah, roaring into Illinois, he knew he'd been only half-right about himself. He hadn't left Maxine behind, not in his guilt, the final Should of all the Shoulds that left footprints on his identity ever since he could recall being himself. First had been the Nate Jaspers his folks had in mind when they named him, and their tent-meeting faith in a Jesus so Americanized, southernized, simplified that, at eight, Nate thought Jesus must have been born somewhere near Cottonton on the Chattahoochee, separating Alabama and Georgia.

The Chattahoochee must have been the River Jordan, he thought, at ten, when he went to Cottonton to bury his dad's father, a preacher like Nate's dad. Like Nate was supposed to become and did become. Sure, of course, his young mind reasoned, Jews wandered around Florida for forty years, crossed over Georgia, settled in Alabama and then Indians showed up. Jews just had different names for places. And right there on the Chattahoochee, John the

Baptist poured muddy water on the son of the creator of the universe.

Nate and Maxine, she a year younger and a distant cousin, caught frogs there, shoved plastic straws up their asses and blew air into them. And watched the blueprint of their lives develop around them, formed by the Bible, by relatives and rules for living and thinking that made all things, even love, a pre-ordained pattern deeper than the ruts in the road leading to his grandfather's home.

*

Nate rode from Highway 24 to 57 south of Marion, Illinois, up to Champaign-Urbana, over to Bloomington, and Peoria, crossed the Mississippi River into Davenport. Looking around, filling his Harley in Cedar Rapids, he knew the South was not far enough behind. He could still smell in his heart the peanut farms, cotton fields, steel and pulp mills. The same attitude behind them that insisted the Past was chosen by God Himself to mold any Present; that no one had a right to question tradition; that love had rules for loving, not honest feelings.

He and Maxine followed those rules for love. They led to marriage; she became a young preacher's wife. They tried to have children. Every time they made love it seemed her family and his family watched, examining his sperm wander through her channels without finding an egg to make "fecund." Like dead salmon, his sperm washed from her body, back to the ocean where they rotted.

And, as he and Maxine faced each other each new day for ten years, they knew, without a child, they had nothing in common except their pasts, the South, expanded frogs, and Eternal Truth.

"God's will," Maxine said quietly, brushed her hair, wearing a cotton nightgown, sitting in front of her mirror.

Nate suggested they adopt a child. Maxine wanted her own child.

"You don't *own* kids," Nate told her, tried to reason with her womb.

"If an orphan shows up on our porch, I'll know it's God's will and adopt," she said. "Otherwise, I'm not gonna tinker with His Plan."

They made love less and less; once a month, then a few times a year. Last year they made love once. Nate took graduate courses in English literature to improve his sermons and give himself something to think about besides saving souls, the Final Coming and procreation. He discovered a world of seeing and feeling in poetry that he never knew existed. Rather, one he knew faintly as existing, but until then he'd thought it was evil; the human mystery, sighed in poetry, having nothing to do with sin. That, surely, was the greatest of sins. This awareness confused him. He had no idea, since leaving childhood, how to appreciate existence without viewing life as a duel with Sin.

William Blake wrote about seeing the world, the whole world of stars, Mars, Mercury and minnows, in a grain of sand. The more excited Nate became by such words, while he completed his Master's degree, the more impotent he became. It didn't matter; he didn't need to be aroused, except once or a few times a year, with Maxine. But when he felt the limpness between his thighs, he sensed a connection between being able to produce children and inventing unassailable truth in a Bible, in an eternal story. The Jaspers preachers had lots of children.

Near the Black Hills of South Dakota, Mt. Rushmore's busts of four Presidents stared skyward, above him, surrounded as he was by a busload of tourists from Michigan. He grasped something basic about phallic truth upon which men who invent gods base their conviction; their erections.

His love for Jesus grew immensely. Somehow, Jesus spoke words to believe in but never, they say, made love to a woman, produced no offspring. He felt close to Jesus while Washington, Jefferson, Lincoln and Teddy Roosevelt stared at tourists beside him. All those men, carved in stone, had erections and reproduced. So had Abraham and Moses. And King David. So had Mohammed. So had Gautama before becoming Buddha. The Hindu Brahman, or whatever they called Him, produced Avatars, incarnations, in the form of Vishnu or the destructive Goddess, Kali. All these holy men fucked their brains out at some time. Spawned. Truth rushed from their erections, fertilized all those mothers, and produced words that could guide Mankind to eternity. Words formed the way William Blake formed words. Words as offspring of the male mind, the male phallus, the absent womb in a man becoming "fecund," his father's word for conception; through a man's own words.

"Maxine isn't fecund, son," his father said.

"Stay away from that man on the motorcycle," a mother warned her child behind him. "One of those Hell's Angels bikers. Going to that biker party near Rapid City. They take drugs."

Not yet far enough north.

He had two thousand dollars left of the two thousand five hundred he took from their savings account. Maxine could have the rest, and the house, the cars. His family would agree with the woman who warned her child: he was one of hell's angels now.

He revved up the Harley, headed west to Montana, then north to Canada, turned west to follow a trail of Gold Rush days. Totem poles and wheat farms rushed by, a golf resort at Lake Louise, miles and miles of mountains. A new faith formed in him the further north his Harley took him, a faith in himself that scared hell out of him. He knew there was nothing in himself worthy of belief. If he ever found something in himself to believe in, Nate figured he'd know it. He'd have an erection the size of the Floridian peninsula. Heart and soul and mind and body would fuse as one. Had he been an incarnate God, he wouldn't need such assurance of inner truth. But he wasn't God. David Koresh, in that other south, in Waco, thought he was God. Koresh wanted to be a rock 'n roll star. As it turned out, easier to be God in Texas. No, Nate knew if he had an erection, he wouldn't use it as a sword or gun or any kind of source of destruction. It would be a source of love and truth. Or he wouldn't use it at all. Not for sex, anyway. He'd use an erection to write words of whatever poetic truth he discovered, that discovered him. Songs of peace, like those Jesus spoke.

Perhaps no woman would ever hear them. Until he trusted himself, he doubted he could ever trust a woman again. Maxine had been his best friend since he was ten and she'd wanted him to follow a Plan. A Plan she learned from her parents, the Bible, tradition, from her womb. Always a white picket fence around her Plan.

The truth was, Nate had never written a poem. Not one. Parts formed in his mind, phrases. He felt useless. He could no longer preach God's Word because he didn't believe those words. Yet, he couldn't write his own words. A deaf mute, without sign language, impotent in all ways except hope. A Harley, his only companion.

He passed a sign on the highway: "Hope, Canada. Next exit." He sped further north.

At Prince Rupert he saw cars, trucks, campers, vans, bicycles, and motorcycles much like his own, coming from the ferry, churning ahead and behind him. He examined license plates.

"Oh God! Oh, God, no."

Oklahoma, Louisiana, Texas; the mother-lode of bullshit. He pounded his speedometer. Of course, Alaska oil. Cars from Arkansas, Alabama, Georgia,

Tennessee, Mississippi, from his south, looking for work. Bringing southern traditions north, to plant like Columbus planted his traditions in the West Indies. A boy scowled out the dirty rear window of a battered van, pointed a toy gun at him.

*

And now he neared his destination, a cabin tucked in birch and spruce woods. The professor he met at the university in Anchorage suggested he live in the cabin through the fall.

Maybe his father had been right. "The Lord will provide," his father said, no matter what the need. Professor Reilly looked up from his cluttered desk when Nate knocked on his open door as if it was normal in Alaska to find pilgrims wandering in, broke and broken down, riding Harley Mayflowers, looking to make a new start. After half an hour of getting acquainted, Professor Reilly offered a class of Introductory English Lit and Poetry to Nate, to teach freshman in the fall semester.

"I've been there," Reilly said matter-of-fact, after Nate shared the outlines of why he'd come to Alaska. The "there" meant broke, starting over. Although Reilly was smaller-framed and no older than Nate, he had, to Nate, a fatherly quality. Reilly had no children, just himself and his wife. Transplants from rural Massachusetts. Irish.

"A good place for writing," Reilly said of the cabin and the woods. He took a thin book from his bulging bookshelves and handed it to Nate, *Weeping Woods*. Robert E. Reilly, the author of the poems.

"A small gift. No one buys it."

"I drank too much," Nate told him, trusting this stranger in a few minutes more completely than any person he'd known.

"So did I," Professor Reilly said. "I stopped."

"Me, too," Nate said.

Nate felt large around Reilly who had the lithe frame of a marathon runner. His paunch suggested otherwise. Nate stood six feet in height, in good shape despite growing up on buttermilk biscuits and sausage gravy, pulled pork cooked all night, barbecued ribs, fried catfish with hushpuppies, country fried steak, now 'n again shrimp and grits, fried okra, and the Brunswick stews his mother made. A little peach cobbler, weekends, after a sweet potato casserole.

At thirty-five, his hair thinned, his golden locks now frayed strands the color of wheat crackers.

"There's a rifle in the cabin," Reilly told him. Nate headed to the door, with a key to the cabin. "No shells. Buy some if you get frightened. I'll be up in a month to see how you're doing." He patted Nate's shoulders. "Like I said, I've been there. Now I'm here. Give yourself time." Nate wanted to cry, hug this stranger who showed more awareness of Nate's inner world than anyone ever had. What Reilly seemed to understand; Nate needed to evolve, whatever was in him needed to come out. Even if there was no Plan to guide what emerged.

A mile off the paved highway rose the old cabin, midst thick needle spruce and leafy birch trees. Clumps of willows sprouted behind the cabin. He smelled the air; far enough north, the air tasted green, clean. When he turned off the Harley, silence fell on him, hard as the pillows his brothers hit him with when they were kids.

Reilly's poems kept him company while he ate pancakes and the canned soup provisioned by the professor. Water came from the stream behind the willows. Amidst the willow was an outhouse, like at his grandfather's place outside Cottonton. In the pantry, Folger's coffee and an unopened jar of Taster's Choice. He'd replace what he used before Reilly came to check on him.

He sat on the old couch in front of the rock fireplace, read Reilly's poems. Reilly wrote Nature poetry, a few metaphysical leaps, not many, as if he feared the lessons of Nature would be reduced if a human attempt at their deeper meanings slid onto the page. No word unneeded. Nate awed at the quiet man's devotion to paucity in words, to his finesse with an iconic symbol.

> *In the winter of my life*
> *frost feasts on the cabin's windowpane*
> *like cataracts on the one good eye*
> *of an old pioneer.*

Nate hunted for any references to sin. None. He wished for a few, to get a clue how Irish, as wedded to sin as was he, handled sin when looking back at a discarded, useless, idea.

Back on the paved road, he discovered a gas station, small store, and a bar.

After four days of silence, he needed to hear voices and replace the provisions he used.

"You staying at the professor's cabin?" the bartender said, looking at the book of poems Nate laid on the counter.

Nate nodded, ordered a Schlitz, abandoned his pledge about not drinking. He was the only customer in the bar. The pool room came with wall decorations—a moose head, caribou antlers, mounted king salmon, rifles from the Civil War, auction notices, calendars from long ago with nude blondes announcing each year, posters advertising snowmobile races. Antique America, it seemed to Nate. Above the bar counter, a ceramic face, and form of the androgynous Hindu god, Shiva, next to a neon Miller's beer sign.

"Here," the bartender said, reached under the counter, came up with a handful of shells, placed them on the counter. "He don't keep shells for his thirty-ought-six, afraid he'll shoot somebody. But, we got bears. Take the shells; bears don't know a Good-Ole-Boy like you from a mountain sheep."

Nate put the shells in his pocket. The bartender's name was Pistol Pete, got his nickname while in the Army, and *not for using any weapons issued, I want you to know.*

"You believe in Truth, Pete?"

"Sure. I don't figure I know all of it. I do know when someone's bullshitting me, though. I miss Oklahoma. Now, there's a great state where…."

Nate paid for his drink, took the shells, thanked Pete, waved adios.

※

It happened the fifth day at the cabin. Nate went to get kindling to heat the stove for coffee, to a stack next to the outhouse in the willows thicket. The moose came at him from the far side of the willow. Nate froze, then raced for the back door, held onto a few sticks while running like the rabbit chased by greyhounds at the race track his uncles took him to. The moose banged into the door after Nate slammed it shut. The moose stood there, taller than a Budweiser horse, panting, angered. Nate gasped for air, chest pounding. He peered out the window; the moose pawed weeds.

Nate grinned. "You beautiful, crazy, wild-ass sonofabitch." He had companionship. The moose tried to run him over, but safe inside the cabin, the animal became a companion. Nate opened the door to see if his captor would now be calm. The moose charged. Nate slammed the door, tossed peace offerings out the window—sugar cubes.

The moose showed no interest, not your usual hedonist.

The next morning, the moose was still there, stripping willow branches of leaves like he slurped ice cream. A hedonist sinner, who paced around the cabin, aware of Nate's presence. None of this was in Reilly's Nature poetry about Alaska, Nate noted, sipping Folger's coffee in front of the fireplace. He peeked out the window at his captor; had Reilly overlooked destructive aspects of Nature?

Nate urinated in an empty coffee can, threw it out a window that faced away from the moose now circling the cabin. Nate would need to dash to the outhouse sooner or later, situated in the moose's willowy salad-bar in the back. Life in the cabin, once idyllic, became a prison, as in Sartre's play, *No Exit*; *L'enfer c'est les autres*. Not quite correct in Alaska. Hell, in Alaska, is being stalked by a ton of pissed-off moose when you need to take a shit.

Maybe Alaska was another version of Texas? But in Texas, hell was a wanna-be rock 'n roll singer who convinced some people he was God; Feds showed up and Armageddon exploded in flames. In Alaska, Leviathan came in other forms. Hell is where you find hell, or it finds you? Maybe it's heaven, Nate thought, but you can't get out, and it's boring.

Like being married to Maxine, maybe how she felt, married to Nate.

His No-Exit jailer, a ton of pissed-off moose, a hedonist with a huge rack.

Nate looked at the rifle on the wall, out the window in the fading light, at the moose. The moose watched the cabin. The animal looked ugly, the way Maxine eventually appeared, though at fourteen when he touched her soft breasts, and they got naked for the first time, she was the most beautiful girl in the world.

The long nose of the moose became, to Nate, primordial stupidity, like the nosey beak of the South poking into every nook and cranny of his life. Imprisoning him. This moose wasn't smart, that's for sure. What'd a moose have to gain by stalking him? Nate became aware he now thought in metaphors, with a simile here and there.

The moose stomped weeds near the willows, pawed and pounded, in a frenzy. A loco moose? Encephalitis, like the bug in brains of Cottonton horses and mules? The moose glared at the cabin, took threatening steps, pounded the earth; a rock 'n roll guitar-player throwing a tantrum.

Nate took the rifle from the wall, opened and closed the lever, pulled the trigger. Click. He checked for shells in his pocket, loaded the rifle. He hunted possum and Tennessee deer with his dad and blew air in the ass of frogs. Why not shoot this crazy moose, make stew? The survival of the fittest, that's what life was about, what Reilly overlooked in his poetic musings about Nature.

Out the window, the moose urinated on the area he cleared.

"You, too, heh?" Nate said. Nate needed to pee.

Nate's phallus was urgent, erect, too erect to aim in a Folger's can. He opened the front door, peed on weeds. He closed the door, took the rifle, grabbed newspapers from the fireplace, stole out the front door into woods. He loosened his belt, pulled down his jeans, squatted over a log, concealed behind birch trees. The crazy moose strode, suspicious, from behind the cabin. Nate put the rifle to his shoulder, aimed at the animal's head now looking his way, antler rack lowering. He didn't bother to get up from the log, butt draped over wood, a mosquito sucking blood there for her own reproductive needs. Relieving himself was, at that moment, tops on Nate's to-do list. Adam controlled animals in Eden, naming them, but Adam didn't have to relieve himself in a Folger's can because he feared a crazed moose. There was no moose in the Garden of Eden. Why? No crazy moose in Reilly's poetry.

But here was an insane moose, intent to end Nate's life, in this northern Eden. "The Lord will provide," his dad said. At that moment, he had to believe his dad's words.

"You're not going to shoot that sweet animal, are you?"

The voice startled Nate, he revved around—saw a woman his age in jeans and an army pea jacket. She picked up a stick, took off her jacket, waved them and yelled at the stunned animal. Two against one registered somewhere in the moose brain as unfavorable odds. He trotted nonchalantly to the back of the cabin.

The woman kept her back toward Nate while he pulled up his jeans. "Thanks. I didn't want to shoot him. You saw my predicament."

When she turned, he saw her try not to laugh. She put her hand to her mouth to not embarrass him more. "Sorry," she said, but a laugh erupted, tears began to seep from her eyes.

Nate chuckled, his body convulsed, the sensation felt strange. He hadn't laughed in a long time. Tears rolled down his cheeks, his belly heaved. Then the crazy moose appeared, defiant, angry at being tricked. Nate and the woman bolted for the door when the moose charged. Nate locked the door, sucked air after the adrenaline rush. They looked at each other, assessed their security. The moments of unusual intimacy forced on them made impossible any attempt to retrieve the formality of an introduction.

"I'm Nate," he said, extended his hand.

"Shirley," she said, pumped the offered hand.

She accepted his offer of coffee, took up a perch on the couch in front of the fireplace. She was a graduate student in English lit at the university where Reilly taught, writing a thesis on Margaret Atwood's novels, a writer he never heard of.

"Canadian," Shirley said. "Says she's not a feminist, but her stories seem inspired by feminist concerns. I don't think of myself as a feminist, either, but no man tells me what to do." She sipped the coffee. They smiled at the Taster's Choice jar on the counter in the kitchen.

"I apologize for sneaking up on you like that. I wasn't sneaking; didn't want to embarrass you."

Nate nodded, understanding. "That ole boy had me cooped up for a couple days. Didn't want to shoot him. Didn't know moose were so territorial."

"When they mate, you stay away from them."

"Mate? That guy isn't mating anything I've seen."

Shirley motioned for him to come to the rear window. They looked through the window Reilly saw frost cover one winter, smeared with summer grime and spider webs. A moose cow emerged from the willows, stood voluptuous in the trampled circle of weeds the bull prepared for her.

"I'll be damned," Nate said.

The moose with the rack was crazy because he was in love, or lust, whatever moose felt, trying to get the picket fence up so his mate would join him. Create love-space in trampled weeds, lure her to him. Follow a Plan. Conform. Seduce her with his big rack. Him seduced by her female allure, and her scent, following phallic logic.

"You interrupted the honeymoon," Shirley said.

Nate felt voyeuristic, watching moose mate. No sin visible in the trampled weeds. His eyes met Shirley's for the first time.

"Guess we shouldn't watch," she said.

They sipped coffee, watched moose mate through the one good eye of an old pioneer.

Nate broke the silence. "Probably not. Probably shouldn't watch." He heard his father's voice, "The Lord will provide, son." He thought of Jesus' words about His Father's concern for the feathers of a bird. His mind was not fully clear, standing so close to an attractive woman, who saved him from killing an animal that got in his way of taking a shit.

"Beautiful, though, you know?" she said.

The bull thrust hard into his mate.

"I'm (he searched for words, his heart raced) *glad* I didn't shoot him. Glad you came along."

"The Lord'll provide," she said.

Her words stopped his brain cold. A tear formed in his eye; *the one good eye of an old pioneer,* he wondered? Nate fought the emotion; she noticed the wetness, gently wiped his eye.

"My marriage ended, too, not long ago. A year now, seems like yesterday," she said.

He coughed, held his hand to his mouth, tried to conceal his wound, couldn't. "Sorry. Things are sort of confused for me right now."

"Like to have dinner with me, tomorrow, my place, down the road?" she said. "So close, you can walk, won't need your Harley." She looked at him, not a quiver of doubt. "Nothing special. Soup. Fiddle fern salad."

He nodded, felt a poem form, writing itself.

"You still love her?" she said.

Nate nodded. "I left, though. Had to. She didn't deserve that from me. Where you from, Shirley?"

"Texas."

"I've always liked Texas; God's country."

"But," she went on, "I grew up in Florida. On the peninsula. Too many people there, so I came here, find myself. Still a work in progress."

That's where God's Chosen People came from, Nate wanted to tell her. He felt geography grow like hell between his thighs. They watched the two moose saunter into the thicket, nibble leaves on willow branches.

Some sex, followed by salad.

Fecundity.

At Pistol Pete's the next day, Nate used the pay phone to call home. "Take care of yourself, Nate," his father said. "I don't understand this, son, but...."

"I know, dad. Give my love to Maxine. Tell her I'm sorry. Tell mom I'm okay and that I love her."

"The Lord will provide, son."

"Yes. The Lord will provide. 'Bye,' dad."

He returned the shells to Pistol Pete.

He walked down the road to Shirley's cabin, took a scrap of paper from his wallet, stopped to scribble the first line of a poem.

Shirley opened the door—her in a sky-blue dress, scoop-necked, and sky-blue Forget-Me-Not flowers pinned in her hair. Fireweed-hue lipstick on her lips, a gentle perfume surrounding her—an alluring scent Nate recalled from his first Eden. Maybe like the scent that drove that moose crazy.

"Salad's almost ready. Hope you're hungry, Nate," she said. Her smile was soft as moonlight on the Chattahoochee.

"I'm starved," he said. He entered her cabin nestled in a willowy thicket.

Shirley closed the door.

Behind the closed door, her words flowed, "Wanna fuck me first, Nate... salad after?"

The Madisons of Bridges County

It's clear to me now that I have been moving toward you and you toward me for a long time. Though neither of us was aware of the other before we met, there was a kind of mindless certainty bumming blithely along beneath our ignorance that ensured we would come together. Like two solitary birds flying the great prairies by celestial reckoning, all of these years and lifetimes we have been moving toward one another.

Robert James Waller, *The Bridges of Madison County*

I still have the camera, slung in its tan *faux*-leather case over a tall post of my antique Amish four-poster, next to the azalea-patterned curtains surrounding the small-paned window overlooking the quiet dusty road leading past my farmhouse.

Iowa.

Sundays, I clean the camera, although no longer take pictures. Memories flood my heart when I hold that camera, oil its case with crushed avocado peels, recall the Madisons I photographed in Bridges County, the county next to ours.

Someday my kids, Billy Bob and Sarah Melissa, will discover the cachet of Polaroids that camera took of the Madison men, when I was a forty-five-year old woman, with a romantic heart as big as the harvest moon, and a love box, *so* tight, those Madison boys thought they found an Italian wine press, from where I was born, Italy. I miss those days, now that my skin looks like an eighty-three-year old grape, and Horace, my ex-husband, is dead.

And the Madison men, dead, too.

But I have their pictures.

The muscled arm of Theodore Billip Madison, holding the pitchfork next to his John Deere, bare-chested, wears his straw hat with the parrot feather in the brim. Theodore's head only came up to my breasts, short as he was, short as all the Madison men of Bridges County. I was near six-feet, then, before my humpback hit, lowered me near a foot.

I was on assignment for the *Iowa Garden and Corn Journal*. They sent me around the world photographing the finest moments of roses, daisies, pansies, hyacinths, geraniums, daffodils, lilies, azaleas, petunias and corn. Zuni blue corn was my favorite to photograph, on the Arizona desert, where the sun beat down so hot I felt all the eons of evolution in my blood.

That corn and me, we stood at the end of evolution itself under that Arizona sun. For fifteen billion years, maybe light years, we both have been evolving in the universe, coming together right there as I took pictures of that corn. The thought dazzled my mind, made my head glow with trillions of stars. Me and corn, at the ultimate point of evolution. Me, Iowa farm girl from Italy, who imagined herself a cowgirl whenever she got her *SX70 Polaroid Land Camera* in her delicate long fingers.

At those times, filled with cowgirl fantasies, I wanted something to ride. Ride into sunsets, through meadows of clover, or on my four-poster with my husband whenever I could get Billy Bob and Melissa out of the house and gone to some 4H goat exhibit. They raised prized goats, the jumping kind from Israel that came to Tennessee. Those goats would jump up like a pogo stick, fall over as if dead, come-to, and hop like pogo sticks. Folks in Iowa never saw anything like those goats. The kids won lots of prizes.

And so did the Madison men I rode, after I photographed those handsome men.

※

None of the eleven Madison men were related except through their relationships with me. Actually, there were only ten and a half, sort of, because Wilbur Madison got born without a brain, only grew three and a half feet tall. Well, he had part of a brain, not just a brain stem, because he learned how to grow corn and tie his own shoes.

I sent this amazing fact about all the unrelated men with the name Madison in one small county to *Ripley's Believe It or Not*, and a Dubuque newspaper printed the story.

That's when I got the photography assignment from the *Journal*.

I loaded my equipment in the pickup, left notes for the kids, began the circuit of those marvelous Madison men.

※

The sun shone bright as I drove, sweaty and hot, onto the dusty road leading up to Colin Madison's little farmhouse. He was out back, shooting his shotgun at crows to keep 'em from his cornfield.

"This where Colin Madison lives?" I yelled out the window of the pickup, over the tassels of corn. I couldn't see him because he came so short, hiding out in his cornfield, shooting crows.

I heard a shotgun blast, sent a hundred crows skyward, and my pickup's right rear tire got blown to bits.

Colin come to check when he heard my scream and cursing.

"Sorry, ma'am. Did not see you."

Guess he couldn't hear well, neither.

But he could see, and when he saw my tawny skin, black hair tied with a calico bow to form a pony-tail, sensuous mouth, coal-black eyes, he put down his shotgun. Smiled one of those Colin Madison smiles, the kind that lets you know why you and blue corn stand at the end of evolution.

"No worry," I said." Got a spare in the back. Just want to do pictures of you and your cornfield, Mr. Madison."

I jumped out of the pickup, looked down at him. His blonde hair hung loose to his shoulders. He looked like Robert Redford, sort of, just short. I decided right then to squat down when I shot him and aim up, set my distance knob on the Polaroid about five feet, bracket that with a six and a four-foot shot. Would have the sun setting over my shoulder, put the light/dark knob on the camera right dab in the middle.

Colin pulled off the pickup truck tire, put the new tire on while I sat in the weeds. He worked expertly, unscrewing bolts, screwing them on. Muscled arms, formed from holding that shotgun, I figured, which was taller than he was when he stood up. Veins throbbed in his strong neck, above his coveralls. He took a red handkerchief from his back pocket, wiped the salty sweat from his baby blue eyes that tore at my heart. His eyes pierced my soul when he looked my way, smiling beneath his New York Yankee baseball cap.

"Hot one today," he said.

"Very," I said. I wanted to add, *caro mio*, but...he wouldn't know Italian.

"Want some ice tea? Got some made up. Liptons," he said, brushed a fly from his white teeth.

"Have a beer to go with?"

"Is the Pope *Catholic*?" he replied, with his teasing grin. He knew, in his heart, we were headin' for Catholic sinning, Tuscan-tawdry with an Anglican twist, the kind of sinnin' that confessions were made for.

He expertly ripped the flip-top lid from the Miller's beer, handed the can to me, did the same for himself, and we went to his porch.

"My assignment, to do all the Madison men of Bridges County," I told him while we sat in rocking chairs, enjoying the companionship. Shooting crows could be lonely work. So could shooting pictures of corn and flowers.

"Well," he said. "you want to do *me* first? Why me?"

"Your place was the closest."

He looked at me strange when I said that. Both of us realized at that moment we'd been on a road in life that led to this place, at this moment, on this day, at this year, in this county.

Fate; how Orientals say our destinies intertwined.

He took out his Swiss army knife, cleaned his fingernails. He whipped that blade out so expertly, I felt moistness between my legs. Something about a short man with dirty fingernails, a Miller's, that takes me back, back to my Mesozoic past. When feelings first erupted on this planet, in corn and ferns. That's where feelings began; in plants, long ago, when they dug their roots into the warm fickle earth, reaching for sun.

Like me and Colin.

"Like this?" Colin Madison asked, hand holding a pitchfork next to a pile of corn husks he kept near his pigs.

"Perfect! Hold it, right...there."

I pushed the red button as the sun set on Colin. After ten pushes of that button, my Polaroid pack showed empty.

"Got more in the pickup," I said.

"Ma'am, I tire of holding this pitchfork. Could we, well, would you like to stay for dinner? Some stew could be warmed. Got a bottle of *Mogen*, too, while we wait for soup to bubble." His eyes were clear, aware as I was of what he suggested.

"Yes," I said. (*Oh, yes, yes, and yes*).

He got a stool to crawl up where he hid the *Mogen*, top of his dishes' cabinet. "Keeps better here."

I watched his firm buttocks form beneath the overalls when he strained to find the wine. Muscles in his neck vibrated, like an old harp. His wicked grin down at me, playful, made me feel weak in my knees.

"Hah! Right here, Olivia."

He took the wine, handed the bottle to me. Our fingers touched briefly. We looked at each other.

"Don't fall, Colin Madison," I whispered.

"No," he whispered.

After a glass of the finest *Mogen* I ever had, some aged stew and bread, he took me in his strong arms, kissed me. He kept on kissing. "Been wanting to do that ever since I changed your tire, Olivia," he said, wiped saliva from the corners of his mouth. My neck was sore from leaning down to kiss his tender lips.

"Colin, might you have a *bed*?"

He led me to his bed. It had not been made from when he left it in the morning. We threw off the sleeping bag, lay on the stained mattress. Sun has set, Iowa crickets out. O, God, you ever pause from love and listen to crickets? A trillion duets, Iowa love sonnets amongst wanton weeds and willow. A candle burned somewhere. His farmer tan looked perfect; brown skin from his wrists to his fingertips, from his neck to his blonde, flowing hair. I didn't mind the creeping things in his hair. He touched me, expertly, the way he changed my tire, opened his Swiss army knife. The way he grew corn.

"I haven't done this in a long time, Olivia," he confessed, vulnerably. "Wife left me years ago. Said I was boring, corn was boring, Iowa boring. I don't know how a body could feel that way, about Iowa."

"Your heart got broke?"

"Yes."

"I will mend your heart. I will mend your heart, Colin Madison. Come."

We thrashed on that bed till the roosters crowed.

Over eggs and coffee in the morning, he said, "Please stay. *Please*, Olivia. I have not felt like this in years. Never thought I could feel anything again for a woman. Your body, the finest form of woman these eyes have ever seen." He stirred his coffee slow, fearful of being too open.

"I have more Madisons to do, Colin," I said, tears forming. I wanted to stay, live here the rest of my life, help Colin recover his confidence, shoot crow, grow corn, make love till the sun rose each day on planet earth.

But I couldn't.

I had assignments. And goats to feed.

My life.

He kissed me good-bye at my pickup.

"Maybe in another life, Olivia?" he said, tears rolled down his cheeks to the red hankie he wore around his neck. I saw a gold chain with a cross on it around his neck. His Gethsemane, his crown of thorns, now, was me. And he was a man ready to accept his suffering.

"O, Colin. I hate to leave. My heart; I can't express what I feel. You were so wonderful in bed last night, and this morning in the clover field (though I'm allergic to clover), in the barn, on your porch, in your cornfield. Corn'll never smell like that again to me. I will never find another man like you, Colin Madison, of Bridges County."

"Nor I another woman like you, Olivia, Italian lass with the silky white udders, loving heart. Write. Call. *Stay in touch*, please, please. My life will be nothing now that I know what life can be."

He held his New York Yankee cap while I drove off. I watched him in my rearview mirror, going to his porch, picking up his banjo. He played the sad songs and love songs he had played and sang for me the night before, in moonlight; *Polly Went A-Courtin'* and *Harvest Moon* were his best.

I did the rest of the Madison men that summer, for the *Iowa Corn and Garden Journal*. They played their fiddle, banjo, Jew's harp, accordion, clarinet, and bongo drum, when I left, creating a musical memory of our time, so short, together. Their queer little voices filled the Mid-West night air with songs of passion, days not grabbed, of a woman who had to travel on.

I keep their smiling, handsome faces locked in a metal box I hope Billy Bob and Melissa find after I'm gone, so they know who their mother was, and what devotion to them cost her. I remained faithful to their father.

I never went back to the Madison men, but each summer, I buy some *Mogen*, chill some *Miller's*, get my framed Pope picture, pull out my treasure box, look at my Polaroids.

I wonder if they ever think of me, those Madisons of Bridges County, Iowa.

My brother and me found our mom's metal box with the photos and her writing about them after she died. Disgusting. Makes the blue ribbons we won for our prize goats seem Tuscan Tawdry. We threw away the photos. Hope no one ever finds out what a horny old lady our mom was, so we can have our dignity. Preacher Alphonse Detoit told us, when we took our sad discovery to him, "Sins of the parents should not be visited upon the children; Praise the Lord. May her sins be washed in the blood of the Lamb."

Or the goats?

We got rid of those jumping-bean goats when we learned mom gave us our 4-H project, so she could diddle around.

They are still growing corn in Bridges County, but we ain't.

Miss Melissa Newcombe
& Billy-Bob Newcombe

Yesterday, Mom Had Blood

dripped into her. At one time, her blood dripped
into him, nine months and a few days,
when she was young, and he lived
in her womb.

She willed him to slide from her body.
Bloody he was, greased, aghast
to be hurled onto earth without his consent.

At ninety-six years, she receives stranger's blood.
Without it, she'd wither, die. And he,
his veins and blood, thousands of miles away.

How are debts paid
to a woman's youth, robbed,
even as she found him beautiful
before he knew air?

A Lover's Quarrel

L'enfer c'est les autres.
(Joseph Garcin's words to Estelle Rigault and Inèz Serrano)
Jean-Paul Sartre, *Huit-clos* (No Exit)

Once upon a time there was a Woman-Accuser who...
   Wait.

Before we go on it must be clear she was an ordinary woman, a woman with medium-sized breasts, hips sculpted by ordinary estrogen, and the need in her for creation to slide between them; a dress reaching to her calves, standing on high heels (for no other reason than men made a living designing high heels to make her sway like an orgasm when she walked), with long or short hair, curled or uncurled, distinctly sculpted to her preference for beauty or convenience; wearing lipstick, rouge, and eye paint; with a trapped look upon her attractive but ordinary face...

...*stood before a Judge.*

The Judge, a normal transvestite, a man dressed like a woman or a woman dressed like a man, the truth in this having no point or purpose; and over the clothes the Judge wore ordinary black robes, sitting behind a Judge's desk. *TRUTH BEGINS HERE*, inscribed on the desk.

The ordinary woman was pregnant, and as she presented her case, she expanded, making those in the courtroom nervous since it wasn't clear whether she was giving birth to a baby, or an idea.

Seated in front of the Judge's desk was a stenographer, recording the tale of the woman. The stenographer, too, was an ordinary woman.

Across from the Woman Accuser was a man, one of her lovers or a husband, it didn't matter. He had a habit of screaming in court, or whenever his team (the Yankees) lost, or whenever the woman accused him of salivating at bedtime. To control his screaming, the Judge ordered that no radio, TV, or newspaper reports of sports be allowed in the room, no iPhone or ESPN app; that the man was to be gagged, his mouth taped, and his socialization process not discussed (Freud was passé in courts of law, of truth, and justice). He'd had his chance to scream outside the courtroom during his childhood experiences of pain and to scream at his woman; for a long, long time although perhaps to no one in particular. But *he'd not been denied by society the expression of his views,* is the point.

Society denied her an expression of her need to scream about him. She merited appearing in court, therefore.

The woman, whose name was Edith, presented her case. "He denied me my right to Quality, your Honor."

It was, all agreed, her fundamental right. She knew this was her right from birth on when quality things were presented for her enjoyment. There were dolls, stuffed animals, dresses, puppets, her father's princely self, crayons, her mother's shadow against her life, the limited options for her life, timed chemicals flowing through the channels of her body, her thoughts and fantasies, and a limited number of new-life eggs which, since limited, gave a magnificent quality to each egg.

The stenographer, who hadn't had such a flow of quality through her life, although she also suffered her mother's shadow, wanted to question the court's assumption. But, she was only a stenographer, so she couldn't say anything.

Edith said, "He promised a unique and supple Quality to each day; flowers, tender words, holding my hand, respect for my ideas, the compassion of his arms when I might cry, the touching of cheeks during the last dance of the night, my wishes respected, my mind respected, my sexuality respected. Those were promised, vowed. A contract. He broke his contract, not once, but in a thousand ways. Broke my mind, too." Edith stood facing the Judge, tears visible in her eyes, turning occasionally to glance at the man, Harry, as if he was now an Enormous-Mistake-In-The-Universe, instead of just good-old-Harry. But a Mistake she loved as one of the Mistakes in her quest for a qualitative life.

The Judge asked a few questions. "Were you faithful to this guy? Contracts have two sides, dear. I assume you were faithful, or you wouldn't have dropped in."

"Judge," said Edith, "don't *dear* me. I was faithful to my need for Quality, as best one could be while living with a man. I spent only slightly more than we could afford for clothes, and things. I took up only slightly more of his life than was qualitatively available before a man turns to seed. I held a job; a good job. However, my imaginary lovers were only of true Quality, gentle or overpowering only as my mind wished them."

"Elaborate, if you will, ma'am," the Judge requested, not calling her *dear*, knowing what she would say, but knowing that the man ought to hear her words. It was the man's right to hear his failures, cruel acts, his quest for Quantity, his indecencies to one who had a right to Quality.

The stenographer sat alert, thinking of her own imaginary lovers—Harry, she felt, needed protecting.

"In my dreams and fantasies and waking hours and wishes my body becomes one of my thoughts," Edith explained, hoping that because the Judge was a transvestite there was some hope he (being a he) might understand. "It's a thought, really, with which I clothe and bathe and touch and feed and produce babies and feelings. My imaginary lovers think this same thought as me, lovingly touch me or lust for me just as my Body-Thought does for them. We do a dance of spirits."

"No *actual, real* lovers other than this guy during your relationship? Or during your marriage, or during your WTF?" the Judge asked, motioning to Harry with the tape over this mouth, his forehead bulging, trying to scream.

"Only quality lovers, Your Honor. As complimentary to my moods and needs as my imaginary lovers," Edith said, smoothing her dress with a definitive sweep of her hand.

"Since that might be essential to understanding all this, please elaborate for the court," the Judge said.

"Well, okay, may I speak openly? Thank you. Here it is; my vagina," Edith said, "and my mind, are one. As one, they desire the same experiences. To be possessed or to possess in caring or in lust or in just plain fun. To share or hide or vibrate with the vibrations of earth as it revolves. We, my vagina and I, do not measure, count, weigh. My lovers know this. Their words speak to my vagina at the same time they speak to my mind, words about me, not about my vagina. Harry talked too often only to my vagina, though at first, he spoke to my mind and vagina, and maybe after a while he got confused. My lovers never got confused. They knew so, so much, without me explaining anything; spiritual, a dance we shared."

The stenographer's crotch salivated with Quality juices, produced by Quality thoughts of these Quality times in Edith's life.

"He!" Edith stormed, pointed in placid-love toward Harry, who rolled on the floor like a muzzled carrot, needing to rage, "requested sex when I was not interested, which is rape. Emotional rape. A rape of my mind first, since my mind and vagina are one; except for the occasions when my lovers showed me how my mind got in the way. Quantity, that's Harry's quality. Numbers, statistics, trend lines, what percent of women in the *Hite Report* enjoy sexual fetishes. You know what I mean, Your Honor. His attitude toward me was *Another day, must be time for another fuck, another goal achieved.*"

The Judge, ashamed, looked towards Harry as if the Judge felt a need to feel the shame old Harry didn't feel but should have. To Edith, the Judge said, "Your lovers respected your right to Quality? Or they always tried to? But not this man, this—is he still a carrot down there? Sit him up, tell him to behave or we'll return him to his mother. He's had his say."

Just then Edith gave birth to an idea, a mood, a feeling, a baby. They stitched her up and she continued. "Something else for him to quantify!" she said angrily, looking at her creation. "Now he can count the words the baby speaks, the dates of the baby's first steps, first anything, extensions of his objectifying ego. His fucking high school BATTING AVERAGE!"

The Judge directed her attention back to his question. "Your actual lovers, please?"

"Okay. Only quality with my actual lovers. In a night we might make love four, five, or more times; standing, sitting, kneeling, side-by-side, whatever he wished, all over the place, for an hour, two, three; coming two, four, six times in mutual union of lust and spirituality. Marvelous. Delirious. Spiritual. Quality."

"Not so with old Harry, here, uh?"

"Once a night is all I wanted with him, tired thing, familiar sweat, patterned hand, moves, thrusts. Limited. Pre-ordained. No magician, my Harry. He asked for IT too often when I didn't want IT."

"Quantity was Harry's problem, the old dart-board game?"

"Yes, your Honor."

"A question, though. Why are you able to quantify your lover's actions? I guess you have a Qualitative experience of Quantity?" the Judge asked, confused.

Harry pulled the tape from his lips, screamed, "Edith, the *Yankees* don't always win anymore. And *I* can't help that, either! It takes..."

They tried to tackle Harry, but he jumped to the table top, escaped with a leap over his pursuers' heads. He ran to Edith, fell on his knees, clutched her ordinary dress. He said, with passion, "At first I was your fantasy lover, Edy. Remember? Please remember. I, *I*, had Quality then, in the beginning. Didn't I? My fantasies of you never evolved into much else. A dull old loving bastard, who never wanted to be tamed by anyone, but you. You tossed me out of your mind sometime back there, Edy, because you quantified, too. You wanted two, four, six, eight lovers, and I could not, as loaves and fishes, be multiplied. Remember your mind's evolution, Edy."

The stenographer, her flowery center aroused by the powerless and handsome man on his knees, left her desk and ran to him, lifted him to his feet, empowered him, tried to nurture him.

"Show *me*, Harold," she said. "Save your sanity. The world will continue, no matter what. Your sincerity is terribly, terribly, TERRIBLY arousing to me—and my..."

Edith gave her a defiant, contemptuous look.

Harry regained his confidence, wiped tears, danced with the stenographer whose name he learned was *Ann*. Ann and Harry—a nice ring to that. Her fantasies of his passion and honesty, as well as the words of his respect for her professional potential as a lawyer someday; which he believed or didn't, it didn't matter—(let's say he did), laid her open. They moved naked, made love at Edith's feet, then all over the room; he, holding her off the ground, thrusting hard into her. They collapsed on the Judge's desk, taking and giving honesty, and her mind and vagina fused as if intense heat had been applied to metal ends, joining them, and she murmured, "Ooo," and "O, Harry," and "Yessssss," and he murmured "Ahhh" and "Argh" and kissed her neck. They sat quietly, copulated Buddha-fashion on the edge of the Judge's desk-bed; lotus-leaf love; she, encasing Harry, seated on his lap, and together they meditated on orgasm, and their Togetherness (the Stenographer knew). All wondered, as they watched, what the Truth of Ann and Harry might be. She lay on her stomach and offered him another portion of herself as her mind soared, gave up thoughts. Harry tried to think of another position, but he was out of quantitative thoughts. He qualitatively nibbled every part of her body, wetted her with his sweat, adored her, lusted on her.

As they reached the truth of their encounter, and she came like a mare in heat, Harry screamed, "But, *I don't love you, Ann.*"

Drunk on Love

The courtroom fell silent as Harry's truth moved through the room like mustard gas.

"That's not the way my lovers were with me, Your Honor," Edith said, sensing the room shifted towards Harry. "Not at all. That was...crude. Harry's crudity splashed all over this courtroom. Ann fantasized that he pleased her. *My* lovers were different."

"Too bad, dear," Ann cooed to Edith, rubbing Harry's back. "I'll give you *my* mind. Harry is charming, sensitive, and unleashed me to my core." Ann smiled, victorious.

"Listen!" Harry screamed, unable to say anything more due to the hoarseness due to the tape. He got everyone's attention, sat on the edge of the Judge's desk, hair ruffled, energy spent, outraged. "I can't control what's in Y0UR minds! Ann, did you hear me—I don't love you, so the cosmic bang in your head was not a joint eruption. I had mine, you had yours. I need *love* to fuse with a woman. I'm a fantasy to you. Would you two get out of your fantasies!"

Edith only watched Harry's lips move, couldn't hear his words. "You only had *sex* with that woman. No Quality. Animal. Selfish. So limited," Edith hissed.

Ann became angry, threw the Judge's water on Edith. "Don't try to destroy my Quality. Harry whispered to me when you couldn't hear, attentive to my shifting moods and trust and fears, so beautifully. *Ooo*, thank you, Harry." (Ann had only seen Harry's lips move, also, when he disclaimed love for her. Not that it mattered). "Harry is innocent," Ann said to the Judge, her sitting naked and satisfied in front of him, on his legal desk.

"Guilty, Your Honor!" Edith screamed. "That woman is limited in her appreciation of the finer things in life, especially physical intimacy. No one could possibly find Harry, my poor Harry, a man of love Quality in any objective sense. Find him guilty and let's go home."

"Let me speak," Harry screamed, near spiritual disintegration.

"Okay, say something," the Judge said, irritated.

"I'm neither. It's a phony distinction. If minds are important, what about mine? Or else both of them are right." Then he said, "Frankly, Edith, I don't give a damn." In his heart, though, he knew he would never love anyone but Edith.

Ann and Harry left together. No decision was reached by the Judge. Years later Ann returned to the Judge. Harry, she claimed, did it again. This time Harry brought his own tape, slept through his trial. He knew he was guilty.

Sometime later, he died. Years later, Ann died. And, as an ordinary old lady who had not much use for sex, or men, Edith died.

And that's the end of the story.

Cosmic Conversation

*Through Eros's undying love for her,
Psyche became a goddess.*

Myth of Eros and Psyche

"What," the Man said to God, "do you want?"

God examined her mind, her feelings, "Space. I want more space." The Man thought about this, examined God's Universe, concluded She had a reasonable request. Her Universe came cluttered with galaxies, comets, gaseous driblets everywhere, dark holes, and a few spaceships.

"Okay," he said, "have all the space you want. Make more space outside your Universe and have fun in it, be creative and peaceful."

God was not satisfied.

"So," the Man said, "What do you want?"

"I feel lonely in all this space. I want intimate relationships."

The Man found lonely spirits with what seemed interesting qualities. One juggled Neurons with his ears, another ate gas and gave off beans that became stars, still others turned themselves inside-out like gloves from a wet hand.

These were new to God, their originality delighted Her, but they didn't know how to be intimate for very long.

She decided to be intimate with them all-together, to extend their originality as a group since individually each failed to satisfy her. When they all showed up at once, they fought, threw beans and neurons, tried to win Her undivided attention, Her devotion.

God tired of this.

The Man asked, "Okay, what do you want?"

"Maybe a job? If I had a job, say, nine to five? Being God is too much. Everybody needs me; I feel responsible for everything and everybody in the Universe."

The Man asked around. Folks said, "What can she do?" They looked for pipefitters, cowgirls, skills like that.

She came overqualified.

Finally, he found a job for Her; assembling thoughts in a Think Tank.

She grew tired of this. "There are no new thoughts. All thoughts are repetitious—like making stars."

"Well, what do you really, really, really want?" the Man said, losing patience.

She thought about His question for a long time—for thousands and thousands of light years, moving through worm holes, dodging comets. She finally knew what she wanted more than anything in the world.

"To be myself."

"But you're God. You can't be a self," the Man said.

"Can if I want."

"What are you talking about?"

"What do you mean I can't do what I want? I'm God. If I refuse to be God, then I'm not God."

Her logic was impeccable, even though it hurt his brain.

He had to be honest with Her, "You're wrong. I made You God, we all did. We need a God and You're It. You have no choice, that's what being a God is all about."

To shut him up, God turned the Man into light rays around a planet. In Morse code, with light bits, a message came from the Man to God in Her Immense Space.

"OOOOKKKAAAAYY. *What do You neeeeeeeed?*"

In a voice that sucked up all the gases into one solid mass, God cried through all the Universe—"*I don't fucking knnnnoooowwwwww!*"

And that was the end of everybody, and everything.

Light Affairs

> *Psyche (almost crying)*
> *O, forgive me, my darling.*
> Myth of Eros and Psyche

Harry sold generators. Big ones. His generators provided light to ten states. The more generators he sold the more rooms in their home Edith converted into storage and production space for her rugs and tapestries. First, the spare bedroom, then Jenny was born and claimed it; then the family room, then the wall knocked out to his den to give her more space. Now their cars spent nights in the snow since the garage had been converted to a yarn dyeing center.

The more rugs Edith produced on her looms; elegant, rich, artistic works; the more distant she became.

"I need space, Harry," she told him.

"You've got half the damn place now, Edy."

"Not that kind of space."

She'd spend two weeks here and there away, usually in California, sometimes New York or LA, visit friends, galleries, getting space. Her need for space (what he imagined as a mental vacuum, or a black hole in his universe) coincided with the birth of Jennifer and the time-span between Edith's thirtieth and thirty-fifth years. During their first ten years Edith couldn't stand to be apart from him (but had to because he traveled a lot, sold generators, lighting up America), but now she couldn't stand being too close for very long. It puzzled him because he was never very talkative with her, never demanded to occupy much of her mind those first years, so why did he make her feel cramped inside?

Harry thought he lit up Edith's world, too.

"It's not you," she'd tell him. "It's this town, the neighborhood. Everything is so ordered, Harry. Doesn't it get to you? I talk to women day after day who feel good to fit into their mother's shoes. Patterns belong in rugs, not people."

They worked her trips around his sales travels. When she was gone, Harry and Jenn; now five; dressed up and went to the few elegant restaurants in town, swam on Saturdays, bought presents for Edith. Edith returned home exuberant, content. She dyed her hair, streaked her black strands with grey, joined a health spa, read Colette. Then the neighbors and wintry streets and patterns of the days would fall in upon her, she'd hug Jenny, kiss Harry warmly, and run down the loading ramp to the plane, her flying carpet.

Harry decided he'd become more interesting. It never occurred to him that one could not, as with a generator, flip a switch and bring new currents and light into his identity. A neighbor agreed to take Jenny for a weekend when Edith was away in Carmel, and, without warning Edith, he hopped a plane to join her. A mad weekend, he imagined, jogging on the beach, boutique-hopping, romantic dinners, making love. He read a book on the history of weaving on the flight before drifting off to sleep.

The man he found her with in Carmel was Iranian, or Turkish; Harry was vague on that part of the world. The man sold rugs, owned an Arabian horse ranch, and was a few years younger than Edith. Edith's affair seemed perverse.

"I know," he told her, feeling the sadness beneath his anger, "it wasn't *me*. It was the town, the goddamn neighborhood...."

"You shouldn't have done this, Harry," she said, crying, fighting the guilt his look tried to funnel into her.

"This is *space*?" he said, motioned in his sweep of eyes and arms to the diaphragm on the dresser.

"I was beginning to feel integrated, Harry. Not scattered into pieces. He and I weren't in love; I love you. How do you love someone for eighteen years and have any sense left of your own identity?"

"I do, Edith. I have a sense of my identity after eighteen years of loving you. I don't understand *integrated*, Edith. *Space* I was kind of understanding. *Integration* seems like psychological bullshit for people who are too... whatever...to accept the limits of human life. What does going-to-bed with some Persian have to do with being integrated?"

He called her a name he'd regret later and stormed off to the bar.

Harry's anger turned to confusion in the bar, throwing peanuts into his mouth. Is it my looks, my body?" he wondered out loud, looking over the counter at his reflection in the mirror.

"What?" the bartender asked.

"My looks or my body, is that why she did it?" Harry said, eye to eye with the bartender, beer foam on Harry's moustache.

"Probably *his* looks and his body. Sorry, buddy," the bartender said, wiped the counter.

"I can't explain it, Harry," she told him when he returned to their room. "At first it was just space, away from being wife, mother, taxi. The most intimate, meaningful thing I share with my friends are recipes, and their arguments with their husbands. Their worlds come in ounces. *You* can't even see me as a person, anymore. You see me in my roles, fragmented. One of my roles is a sex partner for you, and you implied I wasn't very good at that any more. I agree. I wasn't. I was becoming an interesting one for you, in my own way."

"I can't stand this, Edith."

"You called me a Slut, Harry. I can't stand that, either."

"Is he better than me, in bed?"

The question was so ludicrous, she laughed. Harry threw an ashtray against the wall, the shattering glass made her jump. She explained her laugh, but it only made Harry sullen, hurt. "He was a new; I could be different. It wasn't him; it was me. I opened up and not just in bed. I couldn't with you because I didn't know *how,* any more. Maybe I never did when we were young, but it seemed I did. It wasn't just you, but, *my God,* you've had other women, Harry."

This was, she knew, a poor defense, but one he might comprehend.

"They were different. They didn't *integrate* me. I didn't plan them, they just happened."

"O, Harry…"

He refused to speak on the flight home. Edith allowed the guilt to envelope her—what other way to please him? Harry wanted her spirit broken, her identity from him tossed away, her space wide enough only for Jennifer and him. He had a right to such a world. Why couldn't it be her? She tried to fit in that world during years married to him. She was grateful he hadn't pushed her for information about other trips; the Greek sculptor in Brooklyn, the Italian art instructor in Los Angeles—her first experience three years ago. Only three men, but several fine nights and interesting conversation during the days. At times, she thought it was the excitement of new encounters, the not-knowing what would happen, the delight her presence gave to these men. Trite quests? Yet each experience had come back with her into her loom, and the rugs and tapestries were playful, creative, showing more honesty about herself. A few had been purchased by museums—*MUSEUMS*; could that have happened if all she'd received was a good lay away from the homestead?

Harry had been essential, too, to the process, as had being Jenny's mother. Without all the ingredients in her life, she knew the loom would have been stale, making copies of someone else's mind. Yet, that which allowed it all to come together would destroy it. Why couldn't she want to be a computer programmer, or a nurse? Being an artist was like being a river, always emptying herself, needing to be replenished by streams and juices and melting snow which came from great distances to revivify her, coming to her unseen, melding into her when even she was unaware.

Pushing Jenny from her body had been the most startling, shattering, marvelous experience of her life—a new stream. Then, mothering siphoned off more and more of herself. Harry's presence became more tedious, but he provided something essential, something like the land over which she confidently moved—the context of her motions—and she loved him for that, and maybe more.

Then there was the loom, the instrument of her interactions with herself. When it grew silent, even the air seemed leaden, and Jennifer's new discoveries of life seemed less intriguing. Why couldn't a day or week in the country, alone, give her new energies and hopes? Why these men, these out-of-bounds sorties? Was she, as Harry called her in anger, a woman of limited moral fiber? What was morality? It seemed to be the measure of how well a person conformed to societal rules in one sense—in Harry's sense. There was her personal morality, her rules for herself, and these seemed more demanding than any others. One of her moral rules—never allow the light to go out of her work.

※

"You want a divorce, Edith?"

A month later, a month in which Harry remained more within himself, afraid to know the full circumference of his limitations in Edith's life.

"I don't know. Do you? Can we talk more, please? I don't fully understand myself, Harry, or us. I'm just happening each day, as you are."

"I thought you were happy with me."

"It's more complex than happy," she said.

"You think I can't be complex, that you're the only one who can be complex? My complexity is different than yours. Don't try to make me simpler than I am."

"It's not just…it's artist and non-artist, and I don't understand it. I just feel it."

"Women who can't paint Easter eggs have fuck-flings, Edith."

"See? You don't get it. This wasn't some fuck-fling. It was an experience that put my energies in alignment. Helped me see things differently. Sometimes I feel like one long fling for you. You weren't that to me. Ever."

※

One night he packed two suitcases, moved out.

Edith found one of his t-shirts beneath their bed, unwashed and smelling of Harry. She folded it and placed the cloth beneath her pillow. He left her the house, cars, half their savings, the furniture, bills, ski equipment, stereo, TV; everything except his clothes and a few photographs of Jennifer and themselves when younger.

Edith sold their home, moved to Carmel where the only fog she experienced was in the air, not in her mind. Jennifer became withdrawn, sullen during the transition. But after a few months even her daughter seemed more content.

Harry quit his job (*I've always considered it demeaning to get paid for hours of my life*, he told her over the years) and joined the Peace Corps, ended up an energy consultant in Djakarta. Harry decided to light up the world. Their divorce became finalized sometime during his flight to Indonesia, thirty-three thousand feet above the Pacific Ocean.

Edith thought the Peace Corps had died with Kennedy, in Dallas.

For a few months her loom was lively, playing its duet with her mind and spirits. Then it went silent, brooded in the center of a sun-filled room in her new home, like Harry would when she'd been too tired to make love. It was time, she knew, to become more in touch with herself as she did when married, by stepping out of bounds, irrigating her senses and emotional crevices that had dried up. She dined with a Frenchman who owned a pastry shop in Carmel, a man Harry's age but who kept his sense of humor and adventure. In bed, she felt a panic roll towards her. She felt detached while he nibbled and breathed on her body; in desperation, she threw all she had into the moment. The man was delighted. Divorced women, he learned from experience, could be exceedingly grateful; he could relax in his fears of inadequacy. Edith allowed him his majestic feelings, his delusions; her challenge was beyond the simple task of re-arranging a male ego. It was, she sensed, her sanity at stake. *Be goddamn marvelous for me*! she pounded on his back. He couldn't, though, and she allowed him to roll from her, but told him how marvelous it had been.

He sent her a box of truffles, which she threw out.

She spent a weekend with Raoul, the man with whom Harry discovered her in Carmel. There was, she feared, nothing out of bounds for her now. Anything was allowed and, in her discussions with other women, found she conformed to some pattern she hadn't anticipated. The only peace in her life centered on Jennifer, getting her ready for school, taking her to soccer games and swimming classes. She took a job at a boutique, waited for interest in creating to return.

"Edith. Could I see you? I'm at a resort north of town."

Harry's voice—so familiar she had a hard time remembering she hadn't seen him in a year.

"Daddy's in town, Jenny," she told her daughter when she stopped at school during the noon hour on her way to see Harry.

"Tell daddy to come home," Jenny said.

Harry was deeply tanned, thinner, more relaxed than she remembered. His hair had more grey, his voice confident.

"How are you, Edith?"

"You should have written, Harry. Jennifer could have looked forward to your visit. Can you stay?"

"I picked up malaria. You look good, Edy. Divorce has been good for you. I have a few months off; the attacks come and go."

They sat beside a swimming pool, waited for lunch, studied their feelings. No, she wasn't seeing anyone, she told him. He withheld the angry words he was surprised to find in himself. Instead he said, "I miss you, Edy."

"Will you come home with me to see Jenny? She needs to see you, Harry."

"Home?"

"If you want it to be."

After six months of living together, they went through a ceremony before a Justice of the Peace. Edith's tapestries came to life, richer, more complex than before. Museums lined up for her work. After another eight months, the shuttle grew lifeless in her hands; she planned a two-week art-trip to Italy. She hugged Jennifer, kissed Harry, ran to board her flight.

Her lover was younger on this occasion; Oriental, married. The complexity of his touch and presence brought new satisfaction to her work, beyond her hopes and, at the height of her commercial success, she asked Harry if they could have another child.

He brought champagne for the occasion. They burned her diaphragm on the beach, watched acrid smoke curl into the evening air.

"I love you, Edith," he said.

"Harry, I've never been happier. You light up my life."

Cul-De-Sac

> EROS: *Foolish girl. Love cannot live where there is no trust. You have ruined the one thing in life that brought me true happiness. Go. Go back to your people. I can stand the sight of you no longer.*
>
> PSYCHE: *I can undo it.*
>
> Myth of Eros and Psyche

Wanda became interested in therapy after learning she bought a one-way ticket to New York. She knew no one east of Chicago, forgot she even bought the ticket. While looking for a Kleenex to wipe her daughter's nose at a car wash, she discovered the ticket in her purse.

"Did you buy this airplane ticket, Sam?" she asked her husband when she returned home.

He looked at the ticket. "Your name is on the ticket. In your purse. You must have bought the ticket, Wanda. Why were you going to New York? The flight leaves today."

"I don't know. I don't even *want* to go to New York. Did I ever mention New York?"

"You never said New York in any conversation I recall."

Her memory was very good. Sam learned never to dispute anything she claimed he said or did. She remembered the address of her parents' home when she was five, what everyone gave as wedding presents to her and Sam twelve years earlier, the room where the *Mona Lisa* hung at the Louvre which she saw at the age of nine while on vacation with her parents. After six months of therapy, when she was diagnosed as depressed, she tried to strangle herself with rope, but her daughter came into the garage. She told Laurie she was hanging clothesline in the garage because the clothes dryer was full.

Wanda confided to Sam what almost happened in the garage.

They went alone to Tahiti for ten days, leaving their daughter with Wanda's mother. Sam took medical leave from work, tried to give her the support and time he and the therapist thought she needed. Sam kept the rope Wanda bought at the bottom of his socks and underwear drawer to remind him that during his own peaceful existence the woman he lived with and loved found no reason to face another day.

But he didn't know why.

They paid little attention to neighbors in their cul-de-sac, except families with children Laurie's age who lived close to them. When a *Smyth* moving van drove into the driveway across from them, they paid little attention. Sam met the man on one occasion and that was to warn him not to shoot his air rifle at Sam's dog after Sam saw him shoot wandering mutts. Wanda met the woman of the house once, and that was when she accused Wanda of poisoning her dog with weed killer. They were glad to know the couple was leaving.

A *Harold's Rent-A-Truck* drove into the driveway a month later.

Wanda had been taking interior design courses as part of her self-image therapy, an avenue to a job she might enjoy. She stood at her living room window, watched the procession of furniture into the house, wondering how the oak and maple furniture could possibly go with chrome lamps and wicker chairs in the cedar home. Winter almost over, her illness subsided. It was calming to her husband to see the return of her interest in something, even in new neighbors and their furniture.

Then she said, "Sam, look. Isn't that Kenneth?"

The last person Sam wanted as a neighbor was Kenneth. But it was Kenneth Epperson.

Epperson's red hair, beard, and staccato motions were unmistakable. Sam watched Wanda's face change from shock to a quiet foreboding, or he imagined it. He got up to look again, primarily to see a Mrs. Epperson. There didn't appear to be a Mrs. The only time Sam had seen Epperson was in San Francisco six years earlier. But he'd been present in Sam's marriage to Wanda right from the start and he hated the man. He recalled the unpleasant memories surrounding Epperson.

"There's a phone call for you Wanda," her mother announced from the kitchen to the living room where their wedding rehearsal was underway.

The person Wanda met hitchhiking through Europe during college was calling to wish her well, or to torment the man she was marrying. It was Kenneth Epperson. Sam and Wanda had dated since their junior year in high school, throughout college, except for a six-week jaunt Wanda made through Europe her senior year. She met an "interesting person" she told him prior to their marriage six months later. Then, as Epperson's flowers and cards arrived on her birthdays over the years, she revealed to Sam that she and "Kenneth," as she called him, had been lovers. She refused to discuss it in any more detail.

Once, when Sam was upset about her enjoyment of the seven white roses on her twenty-fourth birthday, she said, "Sam, if you insist on knowing, I'll just say this; Kenneth unleashed something in me I didn't know was in me. It's over. I love you. I've loved you since I was seventeen, dear. What more do you want from me?"

Sam was too proud to tell her the truth. He didn't want her to enjoy Epperson's flowers. Each stem, with its full-bloom whiteness and sweet scent, appeared to Sam as a symbol of Epperson's prowess. He wanted her to take back the word "unleashed," to say she'd been mistaken, that Epperson was boring in bed.

Then, just as mysteriously as the flowers arrived seven years earlier, they ceased. Something Pythagorean about the number seven between Epperson and Wanda, but Sam couldn't figure it out, and Wanda claimed he only imagined it. Seven roses each year for seven years, then, *Poof.*

"Why seven, Wanda?"

"Maybe he ordered half a dozen and the florist adds another. Who knows? Can't you stand a little unknown in my life? We promised not to be jealous of former experiences, remember?"

Soon after the seven roses failed to appear, she received a wedding announcement from Epperson. With the roses no longer coming, and the wedding announcement, Sam let Kenneth Epperson slide from his mind.

The same year the roses stopped, Wanda suggested to Sam they have a baby. Her request puzzled Sam because for a month after she received the announcement of Epperson's wedding, she'd been sexually unavailable to Sam.

She even needed a week's stay in San Francisco for some "outlandish shopping." Laurie's birth settled them once again into family life. They bought a home in the cul-de-sac where they'd resided for six years.

While looking for the key to their safety deposit box, Sam came across a poem tucked beneath Wanda's undergarments in her dresser. The poem was typed, neatly. He'd written a poem to Wanda on the third birthday of their daughter, expressing how much he loved her and appreciated their child. This poem said nothing about a child, only about love for Wanda, for their "magic time" and *"passion-ink writing your name on my soul"* and *"Bonds that free us, but not enslave."*

Weird stuff.

Sam explained to Wanda he'd innocently gone through her drawer and found the poem.

"Oh, that," she said. "From Kenneth. Years ago. It was personal, so I didn't show it to you. You have a problem with it?"

Sam denied he did. The past was past, they had agreed. He looked for the poem again the next week, discovered it had been moved. He became obsessed to find the poem, if Wanda had not thrown it away. In her closet, on the shelf above her dressers, beneath her hat boxes, he found the poem. He felt like an invader when he took it down, but since he read it once, why couldn't he read it again? Something strange about the way each letter at the beginning of each line was capitalized. Something a reader would not notice if the paper was glanced at, not closely read, word-for-word. He jotted down the capitalized letters of each first word of each line. The words, S A N F R A N C I S C O appeared. The swirl in the pit of his stomach moved to his head; he felt panic. Wanda visited San Francisco for a week each year to shop and meet her sister. Sometimes Sam would come at the end of the week. Sometimes Wanda would take Laurie with her. It didn't make sense; if a woman was going to have an affair with an old flame, she wouldn't bring her child with her, would she? No, that was out of character for Wanda. He convinced himself of this until he noticed matchbooks and greeting cards Wanda saved and hid behind her hat boxes. Seven florist cards, each from the same San Francisco florist shop. The matchbooks were from San Francisco hotels. He couldn't recall staying in any of them.

At first, Wanda denied everything, then she cried, told him, "Sam, I met him on two occasions after we were married. I should have told you. We needed some fresh air in our marriage. I never saw Kenneth after Laurie was conceived. What more can I say?"

Words from his childhood slithered up: "Let sleeping dogs lie." The phrase never made sense, until the conversation with Wanda. He wished he never learned what he was now so obsessed with knowing. He apologized for snooping. They agreed to let it drop. That was two years ago.

※

"This is no coincidence, Wanda," Sam said, watching the crates enter the house across the street from them in the cul-de-sac.

"Sam, I knew nothing about this. Why would I want such a crazy situation in my life across the street? He works for an advertising company, must have been transferred or something."

"Why, right across the street?"

Two days later, other neighbors in the cul-de-sac held a welcoming party for the new neighbor. Wanda and Laurie went. Sam went to a hockey game.

"He's here, Sam," Wanda told him that evening. "There's nothing we can do about it. It's a coincidence, that's all. His company transferred him and had three homes picked out for him to examine. He chose that one because of the view. He's separated from his wife, has no children, and thought his wife might enjoy that house if they ever worked things out."

Sam listened, but felt sure Epperson lived across the street because Epperson wanted to destroy Sam's marriage. But, as Wanda told him of the circumstances, Sam felt his defensiveness subside. At least he could admit Epperson's home across the street was a coincidence.

"Our address is Benson Street, but on that side of the cul-de-sac the address is Bloom Court. He didn't know we'd be neighbors until he drove over to look at the house. He thought it would work out between all of us because he loved the home and thought his wife might. I never told him I told you about seeing him in San Francisco. So, you're free to handle it anyway you wish, Sam. It was years ago, dear."

Wanda seemed so calm about it that Sam decided to try her suggestion. He went over to give the new neighbor advice on lawn fertilizer that worked best on the acidic topsoil in cul-de-sac yards. Epperson welcomed him, offered him a beer, asked how Sam liked the neighborhood.

Drunk on Love

Sam told him, "You know I don't like you."

"Well, I figured so. But you don't know me. And, it was a long time ago, the Europe thing. I didn't know Wanda considered getting married at the time. I guess she needed to get things straight in her mind. You won her hand. No hard feelings on my part. She's a wonderful woman. Let's just be neighbors. You don't have to like me. I won't be involved with your wife, that's a promise. And, you have a lovely, wonderful, daughter—I wouldn't want to hurt her."

"Laurie. Yes, like her mom. I love Wanda. She's been under a strain. If you just want to be a neighbor, okay. Welcome to the cul-de-sac."

❦

Wanda's melancholy worsened rather than improved.

She took Laurie from school a few days before Thanksgiving, flew to visit her parents. Sam gave her the time she needed, grateful Epperson kept his distance during the four months he lived across from them. Sam came to like Epperson, and other families enjoyed him even more. Epperson was a thoughtful neighbor, especially to the children in the cul-de-sac. He turned his outdoor spotlights on early in the winter mornings so Laurie and the other children lining up for the school bus in front of his home could have light to play in. He fixed pipes for neighbors, gave advice on tuning cars, kept to himself when not needed or not invited to join in some neighbor event. He bagged the first deer of the season and everyone received a ring of venison sausage at Thanksgiving.

When Wanda returned from visiting her parents, she was in much better spirits. She made love with Sam more generously over the winter. Her interior designing talent was more in demand as her reputation spread. Occasionally Wanda slept with Laurie when she felt depressed or spent week-ends with her daughter at a near-by resort, so Laurie could learn how to ski. Sam would accompany them if Wanda wanted him along but remained behind to catch up on work if it seemed she didn't. Sam was proud of his daughter's athletic ability, similar to his own. He liked the delight Laurie took in what her young body could accomplish in the snow, in water, in gymnastic class. She flirted at age six with her father, wearing Wanda's make-up and jewelry. "Daddy," she told him on her birthday, "I don't want to ever get married, but if I did, I'd marry you."

And she'd give him a hug, and Sam would laugh.

"And we'd live happily ever after, right, Punkin'?"

"Yes, daddy. You, and mommy, and ME."

The following April a *For Sale* sign appeared on the lawn across the street. Wanda became depressed and Sam could not hide his anger. "He's leaving. Why does that upset you? Why does that make you feel empty? You rarely saw him when he was here. Right? Have you been seeing Ken? It that why you're so depressed?"

Wanda cried, held Sam, assured him on her daughter's life she'd never been with Ken Epperson while he lived on the cul-de-sac.

"Then what, Wanda? *What is this*, for Christ's sake?"

"I love you, Sam. Maybe I need another child."

That calmed him.

"Laurie would like a brother or a sister. If you want," Wanda said.

"Well, yes. I'm sorry for accusing you. Yes, I'd like another child," he said, jealousy evaporating with this clear statement of where he stood in his wife's life.

That summer, during Wanda's second month of pregnancy, Sam found a note in Wanda's purse. He was looking for keys to his car since his had been misplaced. Epperson departed a few months earlier. The note read, "I thought I could stand just living across from you, seeing my daughter play, rake leaves with her mom or Sam. I can't, Wanda. I know you'll understand. Thank you for letting me try. Laurie is in good hands. Sam loves her very much. Never let him know. You love Sam and I accept it. You found something in me, but not love. I could live *on* a cul-de-sac, but not in one. Take good care of yourself, my Love.

"Yours always,

"K."

Deconstruction Among the Baobabs

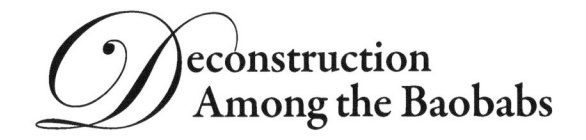

I was wondering myself where I am going. So, I would answer you by saying, first, that I am trying, precisely, to put myself at a point so that I do not know any longer where I am going.

Jacques Derrida (Philosopher of Deconstruction)

LAX reminded Wendt of a sub-Saharan savannah. Tired baobabs clutched suitcases, their flowering dependent on bat-shit and water soaked up elsewhere.

Like his flowering, now, depended. Where's some water? Some California bat-shit?

Over the phone, he rented a cheap efficiency unit. At that rate, he could send his ex-wife the money needed for his daughter's needs, his wife's, buy food, cover film school expenses at USC, and keep his car gassed for the ten-mile trips north.

"Walking distance from the beach?" he asked, over the phone.

"Yes, Dr. Wendt," the woman said, who managed the unit.

※

The manager waited, without expression, in front of the walk-down basement unit of a three-story concrete complex. Neat lawns greened the grounds beneath tree-lined streets in a mixed-ethnic neighborhood. A sari-clothed mother herded her children, like goats, into the next-door complex.

No windows in his apartment except on the sliding-glass door to the small patio, next to the metal door the manager unlocked. Stench rushed from the room, reminded him of biology class his sophomore year in high school; and Julene Lutgen. Julene agreed to dissect their frogs. Formaldehyde. Their high school alumni newspaper reported that Julene was as dead as the frogs and requested donations for a scholarship in her name. He sent a donation to the nuns who ran the school, asked the whereabouts of Sister Mary Judith, his drama teacher. Dead, also.

"Something die here?" Wendt said when the property manager shoved open the glass doors to a small, below-ground patio.

"New-carpet odor," she said, pressed flat the rental agreement papers on the kitchen counter-top. The furniture had no features in common other than chips, dime-sized holes, and garage-sale quality.

"A storage room till we cleared out this apartment last month," she said. "Air it a few days and…" her sentence stopped when he handed the pen back to her. She smiled, clutched his rental check with bright red fingernails, smoothed her hair, hurried away. She strode, he noted, like a used-car salesman after handing over keys to a Yugo.

Wendt shut the door, sat down, lay back on the sofa, fell asleep. He hoped he'd discover when he woke this was an unpleasant dream, Madeleine and Ricki would wave a greeting when he drove home after work.

※

Madeleine stood nude near the open window, hand on a wood shutter, peeked at the street below. "Women with baskets on their heads," she said to Wendt, still resting in bed after sweating sleepless through their first night in North Africa.

"Taking unbaked dough to ovens, wearing veils, for Christ's sake."

Madeleine had a honeymoon voice, a prairie meadowlark in love with a morning. Her voice called Wendt to worship at Love's Alcove while the Muezzin called others to prayer, that morning in Casablanca.

Novelty delighted Madeleine. He rolled over to sleep, knowing their week-old marriage was secure while Madeleine had her novelty. Hers was, also, a voice in love with him, in love with this idea they would craft called marriage. That was fifteen years ago; Madeleine, twenty-three. The idea resulted in Ricki. Wendt wanted to see his daughter more than twice a year, needed to see her more than he needed the comfortable trappings of a man at middle-age. His dream shifted to Ricki, living with her mother in San Francisco where Madeleine was finding herself, her description of her need when she left.

Wendt never suspected Madeleine was lost, till she told him last year.

Marriage had been Madeleine's idea, he recalled, when he woke to the smell of death in his apartment. Having a child was her idea, too, one he'd waited for her to have for eight years of marriage.

Then separation, maybe a divorce, also her idea.

Madeleine had good ideas.

But few of them, he discovered, belonged together.

Cockroaches waited to munch toothpaste and scum in the windowless bathroom. He turned on hot water, ignored rust on shower stall metal.

Drying off, later, a toilet flushed in the apartment above.

Water dripped on his computer, on the dining table. He moved the computer.

"Fuck me," he sighed, resigned to it all, unpacked two suitcases.

He put a beach towel on the table to soak up the sound of dripping toilet water. Thought of Celeste, the young woman he spent a week with, her memory woven into the cloth. He'd need a beach to continue the meditation she taught him.

Where's the damn beach?

"About a half mile," his neighbor in Unit A said, Ray Booth, a young black man from Philadelphia, bass guitar hanging from a shoulder strap. "Never actually been on the beach," Ray said, tuning the guitar. "Meet friends at a bar near the beach, after studio sessions. They told me there's a beach. You like to swim?"

Ray said his mother and sister in Philly feared he'd get mugged in California. Tall, quiet, well-dressed; he reminded Wendt of self-assured, respectful, African students he met during dissertation research at the University in Nairobi. He wondered if Ray knew anything about Africa.

"If I practice too loud, just say so, man," Ray said.

Wendt told him he wouldn't be around much, except nights.

"Bernice tell you what happened in your apartment last week?" Ray said. He referred to the unit manager.

"No. Something happen?"

"I never knew the guy. Met him once. Did tattoos, from Chicago. A black dude. When he didn't come out for a week, I called Bernice. They found him, needle in his arm."

Wendt blinked, his voice squeaked. "A tattoo artist *OD'd* in my apartment?"

"Removed his body a few days before you arrived. Man-o-man; cops, ambulance. Body decomposed. I never told my mom, she'd want me, you know, *home*. As if we don't have those dudes in Philly."

※

Madeleine seemed to Wendt a well-groomed, focused, bright, loving, 60s-nymph.

Now she seemed a focused, bright, 80s-nut. Somehow, her metamorphosis in her thirties lead him down a trail that included a psychiatrist, being torn away from his daughter, a stale taste for his university lectures, and renting a room reeking of a tattoo artist's corpse. Not yet the time to panic about his daughter's future. The solid, grounded, part of Madeleine's newly evolved psyche was her mother part. She took good care of Ricki. Somehow, Ricki was, to Madeleine—Madeleine herself. A kind of *My-Daughter, Myself* or a woman's view Maury Wendt couldn't make sense of.

Ricki was Madeleine's priority, as well as finding herself. Perhaps they were the same priority?

Wendt had been Madeleine's priority for their years together before Ricki. Wendt felt well cared-for till he received the news Madeleine needed to find herself.

During her first year away from him, five years ago at an art school, with Ricki, she told him, *Maury, the world's become deconstructed.*

"So?"

"*I'm* not deconstructed, that's what!" she shrieked over the phone. "And I have to be if I'm going to be an artist!"

Madeleine hated to be out of style.

Wendt flew every few weeks for two semesters to see them. With Ronald Reagan spouting the glories of American family in the 80s, and the stock market soaring, Madeleine set about becoming a deconstructed woman.

She cut her long auburn curls, wore a china-bowl style hair. Dresses gave way to ripped jeans; she rarely wore make-up, gained a little weight, yawned when they made love.

Looking back, Wendt understood what became deconstructed.

"A whole *fucking* way of life," he told his psychiatrist.

"You just lost control of the situation, Maury," said the psychiatrist with the garbanzo bean complexion. He gave Maury a prescription for anti-depressants. The pills quieted his neuro-receptors, made it impossible for Wendt to feel anything.

Until he lay on a beach next to Celeste, who took him under her wing when she saw him falter, lose track of where he was while he delivered lectures.

"Meditate," she said.

In her late twenties, she'd been divorced twice, knew the emotional stages of relationships, she told him. "Like death and dying." Somehow, she knew more about relational pain in her short life than Wendt imagined even existed. He suspected women suffered more, and earlier, than men, and knew how to grow from that pain. He thought of his daughter, his mother, sisters. Had they all been in pain he'd been blissfully unaware of?

If so, *why*? Did women hope for more, earlier? Was that why they knew so much, so soon, about how to handle pain?

"Were you deconstructed twice?" he asked her.

"No, no, no; just divorced twice. Not the end of the world. Throw away those pills and meditate. Get spiritual. The only way, believe me, when love leaves."

He had no idea what to meditate on.

Celeste's tanned flesh-hills, lying next to him, were no help with his spiritual quest. He decided to meditate on circles: a white one and a circle of what he thought of as Dark Matter. He brought the two circles together. After twenty minutes of staring at the circle in his head, peace rooted in his brain. The dull ache vanished. Meditation made his universe serene; *Jesus-Fucking-Christ;* Celeste was right.

She said, cuddled against him, "After you're ready to fly on your own, you'll leave me."

Her freckles bobbed on her nose. They both understood, after volleying possible futures, that the affection and trust which his misery allowed to develop between them had limits.

Wendt protested. He felt love for Celeste.

Celeste had to move on, her project of reconstructing him was completed. He was on his way to recovery. He agreed, it was the right decision, she had her own life to discover.

Lefty and Lulu served as instructors in his film-school class at USC.

The class met twice a week; from three to five in the afternoon, and one evening from seven pm till whenever. Lefty was right-handed, short, balding; a fan of Clint Eastwood spaghetti westerns.

Lulu was younger, articulate.

Lefty told the class he valued Lulu's artistic sentiments regarding film even though it was obvious he didn't think Lulu knew a tinker's damn about what brought moviegoers to a theatre. Lulu proudly said she wore size 16 designer dresses. She tied bright silk scarfs around her neck, managed to be unfashionably corpulent yet nurturing at the same time of body image-conscious USC film students wanting to become directors.

"What does that scene *mean*?" Lulu queried each Spielberg hopeful.

Lefty interrupted, "If we must think what it *means*, Lulu, it's not filmic."

Wendt looked at his young classmates while Lulu and Lefty debated, glimpsed why Hollywood could not make up its mind whether the industry was an art form or a celluloid version of an expensive Tupperware party.

Wendt came prepared to work on his own deconstruction. Learn how to become a modern man, a visual artist, take his first steps in this industry, stories crowding his brain wanting expression. Perhaps he'd earn additional income needed to keep himself, Madeleine, and their daughter afloat. A professor's salary couldn't do that. Not the way Madeleine spent money, even in separation. He sold their home, gave the profits to Madeleine. Ricki's private school cost a few hundred a month. Madeleine was now in graduate art school.

Whatever else it was, *Deconstruction was expensive.*

He subscribed to *Ms* magazine to learn how to make sense of the feminism Madeleine wore as a breastplate for anti-phallic wars. Women disagreed, he learned, and trash-talked each other—*You envious Bitch, Capitalist slave. Dumb Housewife-Whore.*

Etc.

No old or new cosmic roots for being human, man and woman, were safe from root-rot.

"Should we call you Dr. Wendt or…?" Lefty asked during the first meeting with the class, concerned that a man older than himself should feel comfortable.

"No one calls me that at my university," Wendt told the class. "Maury will do."

Strange to be a student again.

After this one-year leave, he'd return to his tasks, refreshed, be with Ricki once a month.

Lefty and Lulu gave him a partner in the class: Rashad, a Harvard Law School graduate. They'd confer on film assignments. Rashad's Persian mother came from India; father, a white Houston oilman. Well-groomed, Wendt noted, linear as a ruler and profoundly insecure.

"I want fame," Rashad confessed to Wendt. "And chicks. Women go for film directors."

"Really?" Wendt said. "What kind of women?"

Wendt hoped the question would lead Rashad to wisdom.

Questions were all Wendt mastered.

Perhaps the women in class were the kind to which Rashad referred. Wendt studied the students while Lefty and Lulu wound five-minute film assignments into the projector during Thursday night class. The quiet, innocently voluptuous Greek girl silenced them with her film about a young woman's sexual fantasies. She acted in her film.

My, god, thought Wendt, watching Simone act in her film, *would Ricki have these fantasies when she was twenty?*

Simone, the Greek girl, came from Atlanta, spoke with a soft southern accent. Black hair outlined a porcelain face that scarcely revealed what flowed in her mind. She used her body in the film to hint at the murmurings coursing through her limbs. Wendt understood, in a flash, while Simone absorbed the nervous silence of the class; she was born *after* the deconstruction occurred, nothing in Simone needed deconstructing.

Was that it? Simone came into the world deconstructed?

Wendt handed in his own no-dialogue, short film assignment.

After the viewing, Lefty said, "Anyone have the foggiest damn idea what Maury's film's about?"

Lulu shook her head, smiled at Wendt. Maury didn't know if the headshake meant Wendt was hopeless, as Lefty thought, or Lulu thought Lefty was hopeless.

Drunk on Love

An earnest, sandal-shoed student named Timothy McKuen, who'd join the Israeli freedom fighters at semester's end, raised his hand.

"The dame, the woman in Maury's film, dove in the swimming pool and killed herself. Jilted by the guy in the photograph she looked at. I don't know why her panties floated in the pool after she dove in. I mean, how'd they come off?"

Wendt winced.

Lefty said, "Good question. I wondered that myself. Anyone else?"

Simone, said, "No, not suicide. She melted."

"Melted!" Lefty said. "Women don't melt when they dive in swimming pools."

"A symbol," Lulu said.

"What's a symbol?" Lefty said.

Lulu said, "The woman dives, there's a bubbling in the water. Maury, you use dry-ice after the cut from the woman's dive in the water?"

"But I didn't see her melt!" Lefty said. "Symbol! You can use symbols at UCLA. Coppola uses symbols. We don't use symbols at USC. We show the audience what they're supposed to know."

"I saw what happened," Simone said, glanced protectively at Wendt. "Love destroyed her. Erotic, passionate love melted her."

Wendt felt hope dry the sweat on his forehead.

"Maury, is that what you intended with all that foamy bubbling in the swimming pool?" Lefty said.

"Ummm," Wendt said, not wishing to make Lefty look stupid, who assigned a grade at semester's end that determined whether he could continue in the program.

"Guess I could have done it better. The hot sun, after the shot of the photo, I..."

"Show it next time."

Lulu gave Wendt a nurturing glance.

Simone rubbed her bare arms wrapped loosely under her ample bosom. She spread her jean-wrapped legs, directly across from Wendt, let her eyes look into his. Wendt shook his head to clear the vision, thought protectively of his daughter who'd fly to LA for their first weekend together. This world had been forced on him, came new to him. He wondered if he'd been walking around in a middle-aged stupor. Difficult to imagine all this swirled around his married world for fifteen years.

Ricki released the Flight Attendant's hand, ran to her father's arms.

"Daddy!"

Her stuffed *Pooh Bear* rubbed Wendt's neck when she hugged him, on his knees. The stuffed animal had been a more secure part of her life than he had. He picked her up; they talked and laughed to baggage claim, discarding what separation and a pending divorce meant in their lives.

On the drive from LAX to Santa Monica, Wendt prepared her for where he lived. During her first years, she had her own room, white lace curtains on windows that he hung for her, a cedar-fenced backyard he built for their golden retriever, a new home in a suburban cul-de-sac.

When Ricki saw where he lived, she said, "Oh. Well, daddy, I like it. I really like it."

Her face, oval, surrounded by palomino hair, shined on him. She was already expert in calming a man's fears of inadequacy.

"You like it, honey? It smells."

"Who cares? Daddy, can we go to Disneyland?"

"Tomorrow okay?" he said, crammed her small suitcase in the only closet of his unit. He explained he had a film assignment due after she left. The only way to make a film—shoot one while she visited. About a girl, very poor, sneaking into Disneyland. Would she be his actress?

Her eyes danced.

In her eyes, he saw the excitement of her mom's; before Madeleine's meadowlark voice drained to a caw.

"Yes! If it's easy, daddy, and you show me how. Can Pooh come?"

All Lefty said about his film was "Cute. But I don't see *you* in that film, Maury. You have to reveal yourself or a film has no edge."

Maury wanted to scream. Lefty didn't see the week before and after Ricki visited how he ate cheese sandwiches washed down with tap water, three times a day, to afford the plane ticket, Disneyland rides, dinner Ricki enjoyed at a fancy restaurant, and film supplies to complete his assignment.

Simone came to his rescue.

"Maury showed a girl experiencing freedom. She called a taxi, convinced the driver to not charge for the trip, snuck into her fantasy world at Disneyland. Seems to me it shows the filmmaker believes in something important about being female."

"What?" Lefty wanted to know.

"We're not dependent," Simone said. "Even when we're poor and young."

Her quiet Jaguar eyes tore into Wendt. He knew he couldn't hide from her anymore.

During the class break, Wendt shared French fries with Simone at the McDonald's across the street. She told him her mother would visit next week, and she, too, would be hard-pressed to find time to complete an assignment.

"Maybe I could get my mother to act in a film, like you did with your daughter. My mom's a director in Atlanta, split from my father. Checking up on me. Seeing if I might, you know, have more talent than she has."

He took her hand protectively in his when they ran cross the street to the campus.

"You want to take me home after class?" she said.

"Why? You need a ride?"

"We all need a ride, somewhere. No, I have a car." Simone kissed his cheek.

***

His understanding of a deconstructed world became deep as the Rift Valley he and Madeleine hiked in their first year of marriage, in Africa, when he gathered information for his dissertation on the history of the Mau Mau and end of colonialism in Kenya.

Humanity crawled out of that valley, ants on a mission, scattered to all corners of the globe.

Their mission—survive.

Now they erupted back into contact with each other, ripped apart tidy worlds based on shared ideas for how to live together, worship God, eat, wed, make babies.

Wendt wondered how Ricki adjusted. He had to speed up his own deconstruction to be of use to his daughter, also born after the deconstruction. Seemed a waste—he'd worked forty-five years constructing a successful, talented man. Why tear all that apart?

He positioned the pillow over his ears to drown out Ray's bass guitar next door. Words came: "Adapt or die out."

He flicked the bug that shared his sofa, sat up. Baobabs, that's what they'd done. Adapt. Survive. Live for five hundred, a thousand years. Find water however they could in deserts, store moisture, while their leaves disappeared, unlike any tree he'd ever known.

Humanity didn't carry answers to his quest for wisdom. Humanity was too new on the planet to acquire wisdom about anything. Nature, that's where the key would be found. Look for wisdom from trees, plants, bugs, cockroaches: life that learned to deconstruct, change shape. Bizarre Life, like baobabs. Whenever the environment grew inhospitable.

Like his own world.

He took a beer from the refrigerator, grabbed paper, wrote to his psychiatrist.

"Dear Frank. You're right. Give with the wind or snap. Abandon the need to be in control. Thanks. Best wishes, Maury."

He addressed the envelope, went to sleep on the sofa.

When the earthquake hit the next morning during his shower and the disk jockey screamed, scared out of his wits on the top floor of a swaying building in downtown LA, Maury crawled on the floor, naked, swayed with the room where a black dude OD'd on heroine.

Toilet water dripped from the ceiling. He gathered all the wisdom he knew, laughed.

Ray opened his door, yelled, "What's going on?"

Maury laughed harder, tears rolling down his cheeks, riding a Disneyland rollercoaster, for free. He crawled to the door, opened it.

"The Earth's doing a belly dance, Amigo. Don't call her Mother Earth for nothing. Want a beer before you call your mom? Or we die?"

※

Wendt rented a bald mannequin named *Phaedra* and blonde wig for his final film, about a married couple that showed the wife turning into a mannequin whenever with her husband. One afternoon when the husband came home, he finds her licking the neck of the black musician who lived next door, kissing him. Simone played the wife, wearing a blonde wig, looking voluptuous. Wendt played the husband. Rashad ran the camera. Ray provided the bass guitar soundtrack and played the wife's paramour. A student named Aaron handled the lighting for the shoot in Wendt's apartment.

Wendt had agreed to sell his Audi to Aaron when the gear shift came off while Wendt drove. Aaron said he'd meet Wendt at *The Body Shop* after they shot the film, where he and his buddies went on Saturday nights, to sign over papers to the car. *The Body Shop* turned out to be a strip club. A young woman Aaron's age, a gold Star of David pendant around her neck, swayed her breasts in Aaron's uplifted face while the men sat at the Tip Rail. Aaron showed her his own Star of David pendant, tossed green bills onto the stage for her.

Aaron's Rabbi father had hired a Swedish nanny to look after his four children. The Nanny secretly instructed Aaron, Thursdays, how to properly make love so he'd know how to keep a wife happy.

Deconstruction, wherever Maury looked.

❧

Wendt handed his final film to Lefty, slunk low in his chair, watched it with the class. The film ended, credits ran, Ray's bass guitar ended on a 12-bar blues riff.

Silence.

Lefty stood, looked at Wendt scrunched down in his chair, did something Lefty never did. He clapped. The entire class stood, joined in the clapping.

"Best film in this class," Lefty told them. "We saw the wife turn into a mannequin in her husband's arms on the beach, then lying in bed next to him. No symbols."

Simone smiled, blew Wendt a congratulatory kiss, mouthed, "French fries after?" Rashad noticed Simone's delight. Wendt couldn't move, stunned by his transformation, his baobab roots sinking deeper than he knew possible, soaking up all the moisture and bat-shit he could for the drought ahead.

Rashad looked at Simone, leaned to Wendt's ear, "If you can't handle the chicks coming your way after that film, I'm here for you. And...I'm free tonight."

"Free for *what*?" Wendt wanted to ask his comrade who stood next to the Rabbi's son who was getting laid by his Swedish nanny, both of them waving across the room to the Greek girl who knew more about sex than anyone in

the room, all now warmed by the applause of Lefty and Lulu for the finest film of the class, about the point Wendt had reached in his life where he no longer knew
    where he was going,
    how to get there,
    or why.

Daughter

A book I read said it must end,
the romanticizing of women,
give way to equality, as if scales exist between people
measuring meanings they evolve.

Does this apply to fathers and daughters?
OK. I'll pretend you are just another person
on this planet we've shared for six years.
What would change?

Your laughter would not be heard
as magical stories in my memory
of a boy I knew, who wished he could laugh
like that.

Your hair on a pillow as you sleep
would not move me to order my life
to care for you better.

Your tears would not carve
an ache in my chest, and your toys
would not contradict my fears
and give me peace.

Your stare, as I come and go in your life,
would not bring me to face myself
as in a mirror of inescapable truth
asking, *What's a man, daddy?*

When you dance, not knowing I watch,
glide in ballet precision across a living room
as if all the world watched,
I would not love in you
all things that move and flow
with life.

When we hug, I would not feel I'm OK
because of your love, and when I tire
of a man's games, I would not rest
in your becoming, as if the silk
you will one day wear could make smooth
the wool I let clothe me.

As night comes, and you are not with me,
I'd not hide from my aloneness
by imagining a union with you
that can't be broken.

Your beauty would not cover
the ugly parts of me when I tire
of my own truth.

What good would it do you, daughter,
to let go of all this in me?

I hope only that my plans
for your life will remain mine
because they are not yours.
This is what I learned
stepping on this new scale
with you on the other side.

When Winston Flats Came to Dundee

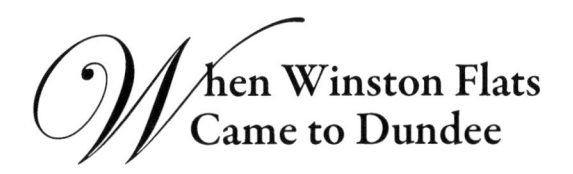

Things changed in Dundee when Winston Flats moved to our town.

I figured our fifth-grade year would be like the fourth-grade, and all the other years leading to fifth-grade. Chumley West and his gang would be the in-crowd like ever since first-grade. The rest of us would be on the outside looking in. That's the way it was and would be till we graduated from high school a hundred years down the road. Things don't change much in our small town, least not that you might notice. Then the boy showed up who combed his hair with a wave in front, instead of in a crew cut like the rest of us; Winston Flats. He wasn't tall or short, just average, but had a confidence found in boys bigger, better-looking than most whose folks lived in fancy homes. Winston's family lived in a home like those we lived in.

The change he brought to our lives began at morning recess the first day of school that fall.

I looked to recess as the two times a day that didn't bore me. Me and Chipper Rhodes would sneak to the other side of school at morning recess where we could watch girls in our class play hop-scotch or stand around talking and laughing. I had a crush on a girl I'd never talked to, but she smiled at me twice in the fourth-grade while we walked back to our classroom, Katie M. There were two girls in our class with the name of Katie; Katie M and Katie B. Chumley West had a crush on Katie M, too, so I didn't have a chance to get *I*

Like You from her on Valentine's candy. But I knew Katie M thought about me from the way she smiled at me, twice.

Our school looked like an old brick fort surrounded by a half acre of asphalt on either side; boys' and girls' sides. The girls' side had what they called a Maypole, chain links hung from the center that the girls held while running in a circle, flying around the metal pole at the center while holding onto the chain link. The boys' side had a basketball court. Me and Chipper got chose sometimes to be on a side in a basketball game if one of the good players came down sick. Chumley West would be the captain of one side and his friend, Spider Bradley, chose the other. Spider was taller than Chumley, both thought to be good-looking by girls in our class. I never understood what made a boy good-looking in a girl's eyes. They felt close, those two, enjoyed being the most popular boys in our class. Also, they were good at anything involving a ball.

I never touched a basketball till the fourth-grade; my friend, Chipper, unfamiliar as me with the peculiar requirements for handling a basketball. Chumley could run fast as a greyhound while he dribbled a basketball, pass the ball behind his back, bounce it between his legs, flip the ball over his shoulder to a teammate without a look. A show-off. One thing Chumley couldn't do well was put the ball through the hoop unless he stood right under the basket. He wore thick glasses, his only physical frailty. I suspect his folks hadn't found a reliable eye doc in town to give him the vision needed to make longer shots.

Then Winston Flats joined our class that fall.

At recess, Chumley and Spider chose their teams, leaving out me, Chipper, and the new kid, Winston Flats.

"You guys can substitute, Okay?" Chumley said. "We need one of you to referee. How about you, Weasel?"

I didn't like the nickname he gave me, *Weasel*. I told him I didn't want to referee.

Winston, the new kid, said, "I'll referee."

"Who are *you*?" Chumley said.

"Winston Flats."

"*Winston?*" Chumley laughed at his name.

"What's your name?" the new kid said.

"Chumley."

"Chum-*lee*? Interesting name," is all Winston Flats said. "Now, when do we get to play if I referee?"

"We'll let you know," Chumley said. "You know how to referee?"

"Of course. Give me the ball, please, and let's get going."

The new kid had good manners even when doing something he didn't like.

A few minutes before recess ended, Winston Flats blew his whistle, stopped the game.

"Time for us to get in the game before recess is over," Winston said.

Chumley wasn't pleased but nodded okay. He let me, Chipper, and Winston Flats in the game. Winston Flats said he'd guard Chumley. Same size as Chumley, so we said okay; no one liked to guard Chumley. He could dribble around you, make you look silly. Chumley dribbles at Winston, fakes a move to the left, heads to his right for a layup. Winston tapped the ball when Chumley tried his famous move. Winston's hands were so quick I couldn't see exactly what he did. But there bounced the ball, bounced away from Chumley.

Winston grabbed the ball, dribbled like an antelope to the other end for a layup.

I never saw Chumley so angry. I couldn't hold back a laugh.

"Give me the ball," Chumley said, angry, to Winston. He looked snake eye at me for laughing.

"I tripped, or you wouldn't have stolen it from me, Winston."

The recess bell rang. We had to line up.

I looked at the new kid in line next to me. Winston grinned. He said, "Meet me after school."

Our teacher blew her whistle; we marched in.

Three floors to our school. Bottom floor for the first four grades, fifth- and sixth-graders on the second floor, seventh- and eighth-graders on the top floor. Each grade got its own time for recess in the morning, but in afternoons all grades recessed together. The cafeteria had two shifts of a half hour each; lower grades first then us in the higher grades. Only times for me to look for Katie M came during the morning recess and lunch. The rest of the day Katie M sat on the girls' side of our classroom, near the back because her last name began with M. I sat on the boys' side, near the front. My last name began with a letter near the beginning of the alphabet. The new kid, Winston Flats, sat in front of me.

When we walked in after recess that morning, I hoped to see Katie M in her line give me one of her to-die-for smiles. The boys' lines waited for the girls to enter the room first. My heart beat fast when I saw Katie M, like it did whenever I saw her. Katie M looked my way, caught my eye. I got ready to smile but her

Drunk on Love

eyes moved away, came to rest on Winston Flats. Katie M gave the new kid a sweet, sweet smile, looked away, looked back to see if he looked at her.

The new kid was looking at Katie M the same way she looked at him. I disliked Winston Flats for that. Now two boys wanted Katie M's smiles. And both better than me at basketball.

Our teacher was as old as the school. Mrs. Baumgartner wore glasses with tips on the ends of her plastic red rims that seemed out of style, moisture building in the corner of one nostril. Students for years made bets on when the moisture would fall each day. We'd been warned by older brothers and sisters that we were expected to keep up the tradition of bets on her snot drips. Mrs. Baumgartner also had unpleasant odors coming from her body that lead us to believe something was wrong with her sense of smell. She was a proper old woman, so she would not smell bad if she knew how she smelled.

My older brother had Mrs. Baumgartner as his fifth-grade teacher and warned me about her rules, how to behave in her class. No talking or whispering. Ever. If she caught you, and she had eyes in the back of her gray-haired head when it came to talking, you got five minutes standing in a corner, faced to the wall. No passing notes in class. That got you ten minutes at a corner. She'd read the passed-notes out loud to class. My brother got caught passing a note to Suzie Lou Moore. Mrs. Baumgartner read it to the class.

My brother's note said, "Smile at this stupid Teach if you want me to kiss you after school."

One rule Mrs. Baumgartner never thought up for her classroom was *No Smoking Cigars*. I mention that because Chumley West's gang included a boy of immense size who sat in a back row near a window; T-Bone Zirkel. Now and then, to show off, T-Bone lifted his desk top, lit a cigar, and when our teacher's back was turned, blew smoke out the rear window. Mrs. Baumgartner couldn't smell smoke, so those in the back of the class suffered. T-Bone could beat up anybody in our class, so we never told on him.

Mrs. Baumgartner said she'd like us to meet the new boy, Winston Flats.

"Make him feel welcome," she said.

Mrs. Baumgartner had us yell, as if we welcomed a near-deaf goat, "HI, *WIN*-STON."

I could tell Winston didn't like how our teacher introduced him. He took a breath, looked away, turned around, tried to smile.

"Winston's from the little town of Lester, on the border. That right, Winston?"

"Yes, ma'am. I mean, Yes, Mrs. Baumgartner," Winston said.

"And I bet, since Winston is from a small town, he knows how to act better than you boys from Dundee who seem no more than two clicks above a chimp in your manners."

Mrs. Baumgartner was famous for her colorful way of talking, and her references to evolution and chimps. Dundee folks didn't like anyone talking about evolution. I didn't know what the word meant. But no one on the school board could fault the results of her teaching methods, so she wasn't fired. Her students won most of the County science prizes.

I looked at the girls' side of the room, found Katie M. She was smiling, but not at me. Katie M was smiling at Winston Flats. Twice in one day and only his first day at school. This new kid got smiles from the girl that made my heart thump.

Chumley West saw her smile at the new kid, too.

I started liking the new kid because she ignored Chumley. Maybe I could share Katie's smiles and not feel jealous, if she gave up on Chumley West.

Chumley and his gang did more to hurt me than just not letting me play basketball. In little ways, ever since first-grade, they let me know they were better than me. Once, Chumley put a garter snake under my desk top. I yelled when I lifted the desk top to get my math book, saw a snake going crazy, no longer than a shoestring, but I'd never seen one before. Chumley made me look like a sissy in front of Katie M and the whole class. I stood taller than Chumley, but I wasn't strong. My older brother pounded on me growing up, but I believed in live and let live. But, I admit, I wanted revenge on Chumley West, any way I could get it. Watching Winston Flats steal that ball from Chumley was one of the best revenge moments in my life.

After school, Chipper and I waited for Winston who said he'd ask Mrs. Baumgartner if he could have the classroom basketball after school, while she cleaned our classroom. She let him have the basketball, and that surprised us. School property was for use during school hours. For some reason, Mrs. Baumgartner took a liking to Winston Flats. He behaved better than two clicks above a chimp in her eyes.

Waiting outside was Winston Flats' younger sister. Winston told his little sis to wait for him, read a book. I could tell they were close by how gentle he talked with her, put a hand on her shoulder when he asked if it was okay if he played basketball while she read. His little sister looked at us, at her brother, nodded it was okay with her. For a fourth-grader, Winston's sister looked fine. Not as beautiful as Katie M, but she had a pretty face, round as a dollar, brown curled hair, wore a skirt, sweater, and polished black shoes.

Winston said we had learning to do if we wanted to play in the basketball games at recess. Did we want to learn a few basics? I looked at Chipper. We didn't care much about basketball. But this new kid, well, he offered to be a leader, and we wanted to follow him if he believed we could learn basketball. Fifth-grade is a turning point in your life. You leave the world of little kids in the fourth-grade. You're not yet in junior high, but you are on your way there whether you wanted it or not. Chipper and me had more interest in model airplanes, replicas of planes used in war, made from balsa wood kits. I worked on a World War I *Curtiss Sparrowhawk*. Chipper had an uncle teach him the basic moves in chess. I played checkers with my dad after he came home from work. Chipper and me also had interest in how to catch trout, under challenging conditions. We knew more about tying flies than anyone in our County, and how to lay a fly in front of a fish.

These were not talents that got you smiles from girls.

"Three parts to basketball," Winston said on the asphalt court after school. "One is offense, scoring baskets. Another, defense, keep the other team from scoring. And the third, well…" he paused, thinking. "Third thing is everything else."

Me and Chipper looked at each other. We had no idea what Winston Flats was talking about.

※

Winter holiday fell upon us, so we had time off from school. Winston found another school with an indoor gym where he could teach us basketball. To Winston, basketball wasn't about girls, fame, or glory. The game to him was about doing your best, playing as a team, trying to win with each player doing his part. Also, about fundamentals, not show-off passes or fancy dribbling between your legs like Chumley West.

Dundee had a holiday basketball tournament for all grade school levels, played in the largest junior high school gym in town. Earlier, that gym had been the high school gym where our fathers played.

Winston Flats needed a team, not just us three, if we were to enter the tournament.

Winston invited two other kids who nobody paid attention to, to join our team. They showed up for our first practice. Farm boys who moved to town each fall, Al Schmidt and Tom-Tom Jones. Both were short and stocky, more muscle in their arms than I knew possible for fifth-graders. They could run all day and not get tired. They never played basketball, just baseball now and then with a barn for a backstop.

Winston showed up with a new basketball his folks bought him. We came with shorts under our jeans, t-shirts under our sweaters and wearing tennis shoes like he told us to wear. Our folks dropped us off, pleased about our interest in a sport. We would learn how to play basketball from this new kid, become good as we could at a game that meant little to us, and play in the Dundee Holiday Tournament. Up till then, none of us thought we could do anything like that. Exciting to think about, and scary, too. What if we looked like idiots when we played a tournament game, in front of people?

"Three things to know to play basketball," Winston told us, our first practice indoors. "We learn the most important thing first. Defense. We learn defense after we run laps, get warmed up."

After running up and down the court forever, Winston told us to line up in front of him.

"See that basket behind you? Your job on defense is to keep me from getting close to the basket. You can't foul me, can't touch me when I have the ball. Don't let me put the ball through the hoop."

No matter how hard we tried, all four of us together couldn't stop Winston from dribbling through us and shooting layup after layup.

"Okay," Winston said, "One of you take the ball, and I'll play defense. Look at my feet when I play defense. How I don't cross my feet when I step back. I skip left, hop right. Hop a little left, then right, forward or back. Ready to go in any direction. On my toes. See my arms? Always raised, makes it hard to see past me or pass to anyone."

I wondered how he learned all that.

Chipper took the ball, dribbled. Winston stole the ball.

Sensing our lack of confidence, Winston said, "A surprise."

From the locker room at the far end of the court strode Minny O'Rourke. Minny was five feet nine inches tall, towered above us, but skinny as a fence post. Rheumatic fever. The fever scared his folks, so they kept him out of any sport, and he didn't go to school all the time. We hadn't paid attention to

Minny. Winston did. He noticed Minny the first day of the fall semester. To win the Winter Holiday Basketball tournament, we'd need a lodge pole center. We weren't good at any position except whatever position Winston played. Winston told us his plan, how to win the tourney.

"They shoot and miss, we get the rebound. Pass to a fast-breaking guard: me. We score. When they shoot, miss, we score on a fast break. Minny will get the rebound and make that happen. Right, Minny?"

Minny had missed our fourth-grade year because of his rheumatic fever. But in that time, he grew a foot taller than any of us. "I'll try," Minny said.

The tournament came upon us, sooner than we felt ready.

Things didn't look good, right from the start. The first team we faced in the Dundee Holiday Tournament; Chumley West's team, the sports stars of our school, and had been since first-grade. They showed up with matching green and white shirts, shorts, looking like a real team.

We hadn't thought about looking like a team. Chumley West brought cheerleaders, too.

We looked at Winston, our eyes asking; *Uniforms? Cheerleaders?*

"It's about basketball," Winston said. "They're trying to scare us. Basketball's not about girls jumping around, yelling your name. Or wearing a uniform."

Winston went to a phone booth in the lobby outside the gym, made a phone call.

What Winston said was all well and good except that Katie M, Katie B, and two more of our finest girls, cheered for Chumley's team. I wondered if the girls knew, before they showed up, who they cheered against. These were the top girls in our class, cheering in sneakers, short green skirts, green t-shirts, waving green and white pompoms for Chumley West's team.

Chumley's team had good players. They had played all kinds of sports games together since the first-grade and almost won the fourth-grade Dundee Holiday Basketball Tournament against bigger schools. We didn't have a chance against them. First time they had the ball, I guarded Spider Bradley. Spider stood taller than others, but I came up to his height. Winston yelled that I guarded Spider on the wrong side. Supposed to stand *between* Spider and our basket, playing defense. I guarded him on the wrong side, gave him an open road to the basket, and we were down two points.

Chumley's cheerleaders screamed and jumped. We were the only people in the gym, so the cheers were impossible to ignore. Katie M, so lovely, wearing a green skirt and green and white sweater. I would have melted right there if she smiled my way, but Katie M never smiled at me. She smiled at Chumley.

Winston got fouled, called time-out. We were down six points, hadn't scored a basket, and didn't have a clue how we might score any.

Winston did.

What we didn't know; Winston had an uncle who'd been a basketball star in college, and a dad who had taught his younger brother how to play the game. They taught Winston how to play sports since he was, well, wearing diapers. And he'd talked with them about how we might win a game in the tournament, given our limited ability.

Winston sprung his first surprise after the time-out. He made his free throw; we sprung a full-court press on Chumley's team. Minny O'Rourke guarded the player throwing the ball inbounds. Minny, a giant Daddy Long-Legs, arms wide, waved them around. He yelled at the kid trying to throw the ball to Chumley. Chumley got the ball, panicked, threw the ball to Winston who guarded him. That happened right under our basket. Easy layup for Winston. Their lead was cut to 6-3 just like that.

Chumley called time-out. When we threw the ball inbounds after the time-out, Chumley had his player throw the ball to him. He'd slipped out of bounds, too. Minny couldn't guard two guys at once. Chumley got the ball to Spider, who dribbled past me. One of our farm boys chased Spider down, stopped him from scoring a basket. They threw the ball out of bounds, our ball.

Winston called time-out.

Winston explained our problem. Whenever he had the ball, Chumley and Spider guarded Winston. Since Spider was supposed to guard me, that meant I should be open for a shot. Winston told me to run near the basket when they did that. Told Minny to come up, stand in front of the free throw line. Winston would throw the ball over everyone's head to Minny. Minny would throw the ball to me and I'd shoot. Minny would hurry to the hoop to get the rebound if I missed, either shoot it from over his head or throw it back to Winston. A lot to remember in a short time, but I focused on what I had to do.

Sure enough, Chumley and Spider zeroed in on Winston when he brought the ball to our side of the court. I ran near the basket, hoped I'd not make a fool of myself if this play worked and the ball got thrown to me. Minny ran to the top of the free throw line with his hands above his head. Easy for Winston to lob it high to him, over the hands of Chumley and Spider.

Minny turned, threw the ball high to me. Chumley screamed, "Who's guarding *Weasel*?"

I panicked, saw the ball come to me. All I had to do was shoot a layup. I threw the ball too high against the backboard. The basketball bounced off the rim. Minny was there, grabbed the rebound. Minny shot a layup and the ball went in.

The score now 6-5. We were down by only one point.

The referee blew his whistle, half time. We were tired but pumped up for the second half. We had five minutes to catch our breath, get ready.

Katie M came to talk to Winston. "I didn't know Chumley played your team."

"It's okay," Winston said.

"I have to cheer for Chumley's team because that's what we said we'd do. But I hope your team wins."

Katie M touched his arm, looked at me, smiled, ran back to the other cheerleaders.

I felt ten feet tall after her smile, even if she touched Winston's arm and not mine. I wanted another chance at making a basket. This time I'd make it, just for her. Maybe get another smile. Winston said the game wasn't about girls or fame but, well, for me it was. Even a little bit of fame, a smile from the girl I liked.

Winston's little sister came to the gym with two girls from the sixth-grade who lived next door to the Flats family.

That must have been the phone call Winston made before the game when he saw Chumley brought cheerleaders. The three girls wore jeans, sneakers, cowboy shirts and cowboy hats.

We now had our own cheerleaders; two of them were sixth-graders. The older girls were twins, wore braces on their teeth, stood taller than most girls. Their ponytails bobbed when they jumped and cheered with their cowboy hats off.

They knew a lot more about cheerleading than Katie M and Katie B. I didn't feel sorry about that, not one bit.

Chumley West never smiled during the halftime break. Their team yelled. They were angry at each other, too, blamed each other for letting us score baskets, stopping them from scoring.

Winston had one more secret play for the second half of the game, a different way to do the play we'd practiced. This one didn't involve me because I screwed up on the easy layup. He brought in Schmidty, the farm kid who ran like a rabbit. Here's what Winston said we'd try. Whenever they missed a shot and Minny got the rebound, Minny would look to the sideline at half court, not look for Winston. Winston would take off for the other end of the court once he saw we had the rebound. One of those farm boys would run to half court near the sidelines and get the pass from Minny. The farm boy would throw it front of Winston while he ran toward our basket at other end of the court. Winston would shoot an easy layup. Winston never missed layups.

Our cheerleaders did a cowboy cheer when we took the court for the final half, waved their cowboy hats, strutted in boots, with their other hands on their hips. The sixth-grade girls' ponytails danced. Chumley's cheerleaders took up the challenge, waved pompoms, yelled. Winston told us to not pay attention to anything but guarding our players. I snuck looks at Katie M when Winston wasn't looking my way. Katie M looked better than ever.

Chumley made a change in his lineup. He brought in T-Bone Zirkel to play center. T-Bone didn't wear a uniform, but he'd been watching the game. He was in jeans and t-shirt, with his short sleeves rolled up, wearing sneakers. T-Bone never played basketball, but he stood tall and would guard Minny O'Rourke.

On their first shot, T-Bone stood flat-footed. Minny ran to the hoop, grabbed the rebound, looked to the sidelines at half-court. One of our farm boys waited for the pass. Minny gave the ball a heave, the farm boy grabbed it, flung it in front of Winston already running toward their basket. An easy layup; we were ahead for the first time in the game, 7-6.

Chumley yelled at T-Bone to do more than stand behind Minny when their team took a shot.

"Get the rebound!" Chumley yelled.

I don't think T-Bone knew what a rebound was.

On their next shot, T-Bone tried to shove Minny out of the way, got called for a foul. The referee warned him another shove like that and he'd be given a technical foul. T-Bone scowled at all these rules he'd never heard. T-Bone knew fighting with fists, not competing in a game with rules. Minny made the free-throw, ran down the court to get ready for defense. He tripped over his own feet, fell hard. The referee called time-out to see if Minny felt okay. Minny looked embarrassed but said he wasn't hurt.

The rest of the game went like Winston planned. Our defense got better, and they were lucky to even get a shot at the basket. Minny grabbed rebounds, flung the ball to a farm boy, he'd get the ball to Winston to score layups.

When the referee blew the whistle, and announced the game over, the scoreboard said 14-9.

We won the game. Our cheerleaders cheered, and we felt better than we ever felt.

Chumley made his team shake our hands, congratulate us for our victory. I admired Chumley for doing that. Deep down, Chumley West respected sports. He'd done all he could think of to win, but Winston outsmarted him at every turn. Chumley even patted Winston on the back, told him, "Good game."

"We got lucky," was all Winston said. That wasn't true, but Winston showed himself a gentleman in victory.

And Chumley West, maybe he was on the way to becoming easy to like.

Chumley walked off the court a beaten kid that day, not looking back to see Katie M stare with admiring eyes at Winston Flats while he thanked his little sister and the sixth-graders who gave us support when we needed it.

"Good game, team," Winston said to us.

What surprised us even more, we won the Dundee fifth-grade tournament trophy. Every team we played, from bigger schools, seemed better than us but we played as a team.

And our cheerleaders now included the lovely Katie M and Katie B.

I began to notice Katie B. She would smile at me during a game, make me feel special. Katie B had green eyes, red hair the color of a rose, a little on the chubby side. I couldn't believe what happened in my mind and to my heart. I fell out of love with Katie M, fell in love with Katie B.

Katie B didn't flirt with other boys, just with me.

Winston Flats made a new name for me. I liked it better than Weasel. The guys now called me Ace.

The Flats family lived three blocks from where my family lived. Chipper lived right next door to me. My home was a block past a house empty for a year, the Haunted House. Me and Chipper walked home with Winston Flats and his little sister that winter after we won the basketball tournament.

Winston Flats' little sister had herself an unusual name, Roe. Her name was

Rowena May. I don't know why parents would name a boy *Winston* and his sister *Rowena May*. If Winston wanted to get her attention, he'd say, real loud, *Rowena May*.

We called her Roe; she didn't like Rowena.

Chipper looked good that winter, had dark hair with a curl to it now that his folks let him grow it longer than a crew cut. A lot of us grew our hair like Winston Flats, with a wave in front, parted on the side. Chipper's wave went all over his head, and girls thought it looked cute and furry, like a teddy bear. He stood shorter than me and his ears grew where they were supposed to grow, not sticking out like mine. Maybe that's why Chumley called me Weasel. I looked up a picture of a weasel. The ears stuck straight up on its head, not out to the side. A whole weasel was only six inches long.

I comment here about my friend, Chipper, because Roe had a big crush on Chipper. I don't think Winston or Chipper noticed how she always looked at him, but I did. Roe figured out a way to walk next to Chipper whenever she could and talk with him. Me and Chipper didn't know how to talk to girls, not even a little sister. Roe was athletic, like her brother. Roe and Winston made snowballs, had contests to see who could hit tree trunks when we walked home. Me and Chipper never hit one tree trunk with a snowball that winter.

But Roe told Chipper, "You barely missed it that time. A really good throw, Chipper."

"He missed the tree by a foot," Winston pointed out.

"You need glasses," she said. To us, she said, "Right? My brother could use glasses? Shoot balls into the basket from farther away than just making lay-ups, maybe?"

One winter afternoon after school, while we walked past the Haunted House, Chipper stopped dead in his tracks, pointed at a light blinking through a boarded-up front window. Someone inside the house opened the front door a little. We got ready to run when out steps Chumley West. Chumley included us now in his gang because our team had whipped him in the tournament. Chumley waved for us to come, motioned to the rear of the old house.

"Come around back," Chumley said.

"What are they up to?" Chipper asked.

"Won't know unless we take a look," Winston said.

We made our way past snow-covered lilac bushes, an old wheelbarrow, rusted kids' bikes, and litter we'd seen but never paid attention to.

Drunk on Love

Chumley opened a door; we scooted in. Barely enough light from the windows that had not been boarded to follow Chumley through the kitchen to what had been a room, maybe, where people ate their meals. Chumley used a flashlight to guide us. Spider held a lantern in the next room, what seemed to be the living room.

"What are you doing here?" Winston asked. We felt spooked and didn't enjoy the musty smell. "There's a *No Trespassing* sign out front."

"Nobody cares we're here," Spider said.

"We need privacy for a game," Chumley said. "Thought you might like to play it."

"What game?" Winston said.

"We'll tell you after you promise never to tell."

"Tell about what?" Winston said.

"Post Office," Chumley said, nodded it would be fun.

"*Post Office?*" we said at the same time.

A door opened. Out walked Katie M, Katie B, and the two sixth-grade girls who cheered for our team in our tourney games. They weren't wearing winter coats or overshoes. By the afternoon light coming through a high window and the lantern, we could see they were made-up, wearing red lipstick and makeup on their cheeks. I smelled perfume stronger than any flower might give.

Chumley said, "You go to one of the Post Office workers, behind those orange carton crates, tell her how you want to mail a letter. Spider'll show you how the game goes."

The girls got behind the orange carton crates stacked about waist high. Spider went to the crates, said he had a letter to mail.

One of the sixth-grade girls, Julie, said, "How do you want to mail it, sir?"

Spider thought a minute, said, "Air Mail." Spider leaned over the counter, and Julie gave him a kiss right on his lips.

I about fell over.

We took a step back when we saw that kiss. None of us kissed anybody other than somebody in our family, which didn't seem like kissing a girl wearing lipstick.

Katie B was looking at me. She smiled sweet, almost giggled. If I agreed to play this game, I could kiss Katie B. The thought never occurred to me, truth be told. But having to be so secret about kissing made it seem like we'd be doing something bad.

Winston shook his head, even while he looked with interest at Katie M, all sweet smiles looking at him.

"I don't know about this, Chumley."

"A great game, Winston," Chumley said. "Girls' idea. Right, girls?"

The girls nodded their heads that they came up with the idea for the game.

Helena, the other sixth-grade girl, said, through braces, "Have to learn how to kiss sometime. Boys in our class are too dumb to learn. Why not learn with boys who aren't dumb, when no one will make fun of us, or tell? You practice basketball? Why not practice kissing? Going to need to know how sometime."

Katie M broke in, "We'll be going on a date, someday, and not know how to kiss good-night. Feel like idiots? School don't teach anything about how to kiss."

"I think it sounds fun," Roe said.

We looked at her, surprised a fourth-grader said anything around older kids.

Roe looked at Chipper. "I'd kiss you, Chipper. Airmail, if you want. Special Delivery or whatever you asked."

"You're too young to play kissing games," Winston told his sister.

"I played *Spin-The-Bottle* at Aunty Corrine's on their farm last summer with our cousins and the boy down the road," Roe said. "In Aunty Corrine's kitchen, while she talked on the phone to her mother. I'm younger than you, Winston, but I'm not just your little sister. I'm a grown-up girl."

"*Spin-The-Bottle?*" Chumley said.

Roe told him how you sit in a circle on the floor, a wood or linoleum floor, laid a milk bottle flat, spun it around. You kissed the person the bottle ended up pointing at.

"You did that?" Winston said to Roe.

"I did. Aunty Corrine told us how. Said she played it herself on Grampa's farm. After haying."

Katie B said, "We'd not be sneaking out, drinking beer, cussing. Just kissing."

Winston felt out-argued by the experience of his sister and the logic of the girls. He was our leader, so we waited while he weighed all the things a leader thinks about when he makes a decision.

I knew what I hoped he'd decide.

"All right," Winston said. "We could use practice, kissing. Won't tell nobody outside this room. Roe gets to play but she won't be kissing me. I'll watch how you kiss my sister. We only have twenty minutes before we have to head home."

A pleased reaction by all of us to Winston's decision.

Drunk on Love

I think that the girls had it planned better than it first sounded. I suspect they talked with Rowena May long before we showed up. I learned boys knew sports, girls knew kissing. Each had something to learn from the other.

When we lined up to send a letter, girls took a place in their line. Helena would take care of Chumley's letter; he went first. Julie gave the kind of kiss Spider asked for next, though we had no idea what might be heading his way when saying what we'd heard our folks say mailing letters or packages at the post office: First Class, or Second Class, or C.O.D.

I liked it when Chumley said, "Ace, you're next." No more *Weasel*, even from Chumley.

Katie B waited.

I asked to mail my letter *Air Mail Special Delivery* to see what that meant from Katie B. I almost fainted, truth be told, when I felt her lips touch mine. Not just touch my lips. She came around and put her hands around my head, pulled me to her gentle, to all of her. She surprised me, my mouth still open.

She kissed my teeth. "Got to close your mouth," Katie B said.

I closed my mouth.

"Not like kissing your gram," Katie B said. "Like this."

She showed me, her eyes closed, her lips parted. I must have got it right. Her lips found mine; hers warm and soft. She sighed, smiled at me, went back behind the other girls.

Chipper took his turn at the counter. Waiting for him was the pint-size Rowena May. Chipper said to Roe, Winston watching close, that he'd like to mail a postcard. Rowena leaned forward, Chipper leaned to her, she placed her little hands around his head, pulled his mouth to hers. Not a postcard kiss, no way.

When the kiss ended, Chipper said, "Uhhhhmm," looked dizzy.

One of the sixth-grade girls said, "You're supposed to kiss his cheek for a postcard, Rowena."

"I know," Roe said. "Sorry about that, Chipper."

Of course, she wasn't sorry, not one bit.

When Katie M came to the counter, we waited for our leader, Winston, to get postage for a letter. These two had smiled at each other that entire winter, and Katie M had stopped flirting with Chumley West. Katie M stood almost as tall as Winston, had a valentine shape head, surrounded by auburn curls that hung like clouds around her cheeks. Katie M's neck seemed longer than most girls' necks, and, though skinny as a fence post, she was the Queen of our class.

118

When Winston came to the counter, he didn't know what to say. Those two stared at each other. Then Katie M took his head in her hands. We knew it was time for us to look away.

We never saw them kiss. Never heard him tell her how he wanted to send his letter. But I heard Katie M sigh *Oooooo* when it ended, and I felt proud of our leader. Winston learned, like all of us, about one part of how to be a man in this world. A part our girls liked, and we would need such knowledge as much as how to divide one number by another or the name of the capital cities of the U.S.

After a few rounds of mailing letters, Chumley said time to go home. We put on our coats, overshoes, gloves. Didn't talk much, now that the game ended. We had to be ourselves again. But we shared truths that afternoon in the haunted house, young truths. Even if we had to keep it secret from our parents.

I learned something more interesting than making balsa wood model airplanes or winning basketball games. Her name was Katie B.

I ran now with the in-crowd, though my ears stuck out, with words stuck in my throat when I tried to talk to Katie B. I had a lot more to learn. We all did. It wouldn't have happened, none of it, if Winston Flats hadn't moved to Dundee.

Chipper had never thought about girls before that, so far as I knew. Now Chipper had a girlfriend. Of course, her older brother watched to see if he treated his little sister proper. That would drive me nuts.

I wanted to write poems to Katie B even if it meant I had to face the corner, and my words were read out loud if Mrs. Baumgartner spotted me sending the notes. Crazy is as crazy does when you find yourself in love. But I didn't know how to write a poem.

Mrs. Baumgartner added learning about poetry to our class that winter, a cold time of year that was boring except the one time when mailing letters with stamps from girls in the haunted house. Her teaching about poetry interested me. One of the few times going to school gave me something I wanted to know. I wanted to tell Katie B how I felt about her. I didn't know what to write.

"Poetry tells how you feel about something," Mrs. Baumgartner said, standing in front of us, the drop of snot hanging from her nose.

I forgot about the nose drop for the first time that year.

Here's something else I had feelings about; winter. Winter was an empty hole, the time between leaves turning yellow and trees coming to life when lilac bushes bloomed. I wanted springtime when I could see if one of the airplanes I made could fly with a rubber band making the propeller get it off the ground.

That winter, Winston invited us over to his house on a Saturday afternoon to play a game he learned in Lester before moving to Dundee. Snow was on the ground, but the sun shined that day.

The game was *Annie, Annie Over*. Here's how the game went. Winston divided us into two teams. Winston's team went to the front of his house and the rest of us in back. Winston's team started with the tennis ball. His team yelled, *Annie, Annie Over*, and his team threw the ball over the house and our team had to catch it.

You never knew where the ball would come.

If someone on our team didn't catch it, it would be our turn to yell, *Annie, Annie Over*, and throw the ball back.

If someone on our team caught the ball, the game got interesting. Whoever caught the ball snuck around the house, hit one of Winston's team with the tennis ball. If someone on our team hit a player on Winston's team, that player switched sides. The game ended when one team had everyone.

But, if we missed hitting one of their team, it was their turn to throw *Annie, Annie Over*.

If your throw didn't make it over the house roof, your team yelled, *Pigtail*, and threw it again. Lots of *Pigtail* yells that day.

"Don't throw at anyone's head," Winston said. "And if someone's throwing at you, dodge, turn around so the ball hits you in your back, not in your face."

One thing I noticed, he put boyfriends and girlfriends on different teams. At that time, I didn't want to be a leader of anything, like Winston and Chumley, but I wanted to understand how leaders thought. How they thought that made them leaders. Maybe someday I'd want to be a leader. Me and Katie B were on different sides. Same for Chumley and Julie, the sixth-grade girl who had a crush on him. Same for Roe and Chipper, and for Winston and Katie M. Even Spider was on a different side than Helena, the sixth-grade girl with braces on her teeth who liked him.

As I thought about it, while the game went on, I saw why Winston did what he did. He made sure we were careful not to hit anyone in the face; it could be your girlfriend. But just as important, it made us want to hit a boyfriend or girlfriend in the back, so they could be on the same side with us.

Winston's team went first. We heard their team yell, *Annie, Annie Over*. We were ready.

On our side was me, Chumley West, Katie M, and Helena. The tennis ball went way over our heads. Winston had a black cocker spaniel named Missy. Missy ran around the house, looked for the tennis ball she'd seen thrown. We didn't catch it, so Missy grabbed the ball from the snow, held the ball in her mouth, dared us to get it. We yelled to Winston that his dog had the tennis ball. Winston ran to our side of the house to help us.

"You've got to tackle Missy, but don't hurt her," Winston said. "That's how I play ball with her. She just had pups."

That dog ran fast, impossible to corner. She loved to be chased, knew how to put the tennis ball down, in the snow, get you to think you had a chance. Then when you came after the tennis ball, she'd grab it and take off. That dog wrecked our game, and it had only started. Then Winston did something I'd never seen. He dove at his dog, grabbing Missy as if she was a calf at a rodeo, rolled over with her, laughing, told us to get the tennis ball from her mouth. Roe pulled the ball from the dog's mouth, and Winston let her go. Missy sat down, her mouth wide, tongue hanging out, breathing hard, waiting for another chance to get that ball.

I'd never had a dog but, if the truth be told, wished I could.

My dad said dogs belonged on a farm, not in a town where they could not run free, so I couldn't have a dog like Winston had.

I liked playing *Annie, Annie Over*. I learned I could throw a tennis ball high and far. I learned girls could throw a tennis ball over a roof good as a boy, though catching one seemed as much a mystery to most girls as it was to Chipper and me. Our fathers hadn't played catch with us growing up, so we didn't know how to catch anything. Winston's dad and uncle had been grooming him for playing ball games since his earliest years.

I caught a tennis ball. I motioned to our team to not make a sound. Don't let them know if we caught it. I motioned we should divide up. I gave a signal and we ran around the house Winston's team didn't know which of us had the ball.

I cornered Katie B, threw the ball off her back. She had to join our team, which she didn't mind. She smiled at me and I felt ready to end the game after that.

But the battle waged on. Winston was so good at anything involving

Drunk on Love

throwing a ball that we didn't have a chance. In the end, only Chumley West was left on our team. Chumley threw the ball over the house, yelling, *Annie, Annie Over*. Winston caught it, motioned for us to be quiet. He ran around the house, nailed Chumley in the back.

Game over.

We had fun on a winter afternoon with just a tennis ball. I began to think about what being bored in winter meant. Maybe it meant *I* was boring, that there were fun things to do if I just could think of them, like Winston Flats did.

Winston's mother had us in their garage for cocoa. I felt drawn to the cardboard box where Winston kept the last pup of Missy's litter. I saw a pup, scrawny like me, when I was little. Black, no larger than two of my hands. "Runt of the litter," Winston said. No one wanted the pup. I picked up the runt; he looked at me. I brought him close to my face and he licked my cheeks. That puppy wanted me as much as I wanted him. I could tell.

At home, that night, I told my mother about the puppy who chose me.

"Your dad doesn't approve of dogs in town," mom said.

I called Winston to tell him I wanted the last pup of Missy's litter, but my dad wouldn't allow it. It wasn't respectful of a dog, dad said, to not let a dog run free. My dad loved animals. He didn't want to see a dog cooped up like a chicken in a town chicken-coop yard.

Winston said he'd think on it. Next day, Winston called. "When's your father's birthday?"

"Next Sunday."

"Maybe you give him the puppy for a present? Hard to say No if it's a present for his birthday."

I said I'd ask my mom if we could give the puppy to my father for his birthday. That became the plan. I went to Winston's home the next Saturday with an empty shoe box.

"What are you going to call him?" Roe said.

"Been thinking about a name," I said, "Ike."

I brought Ike home in the shoebox with holes I poked in it, so he could breathe. He didn't like being in the box, but I talked to him all the way home and snuck him some milk in our basement. He was happy to be with me.

Next day was my dad's birthday. If Winston's plan didn't work, I'd have to give Ike back.

I put the shoebox on the top step leading from our kitchen to our basement.

Mom wrapped the shoebox with a blue-ribbon bow, "Happy Birthday, Dad," written by me on a note she put on the box. The plan; I give the puppy to my dad after breakfast, on Sunday, his birthday. My dad came late for breakfast, but mom had his favorite breakfast ready. There was French toast with cinnamon, lots of maple syrup, butter, sausage patties with catsup, scrambled eggs that used sour cream, green onion tips chopped in the eggs, fresh squeezed orange juice using the orange squeezer she inherited from her folks. Mom showed me how to make sourdough biscuits with gravy. My dad would fly to the moon if he found sourdough biscuits with gravy waiting for him.

"What's that whining?" dad said while he enjoyed his birthday breakfast. This, the only time in a year he got all the attention. He didn't want more attention from us, but I think he liked it when he got it.

"What?" mom said. "I don't hear anything, dear." Ike whined loud like the runt of a litter can whine, wanting out of the dark shoebox.

"That's a *dog*," dad said. "In our basement."

"Now, dear," mom said. Mom motioned for me to get the shoebox. I opened the door to the basement, picked up the shoebox.

I held the box out to my dad, "Happy Birthday, dad."

He didn't look happy. "What's in the box?" he said.

"Open it, dear," mom said, tried to be cheery.

"A dog," dad said, ignoring the sausage and maple syrup on his plate. "I said no dogs in town." Dad unwrapped the shoebox; there was Ike. He barked, licked my dad's hands.

"Cute mutt," dad said.

"Can I take care of him for you?" I said.

My dad looked at me, knowing he'd been outmaneuvered. "YOU have to feed him, son, not me. YOU water him. YOU clean up after him. See he gets exercise. A dog is harder to take care of in town than a child."

"I will, sir. I surely will," I said, more excited than when Katie B kissed me at the Post Office game.

"Don't call me 'sir.' I'm your dad."

For the first time, I threw my arms around my father. We were not given to emotional display, me and my dad, but I felt him relax, and he put his arms around me. It felt good.

"Looks like we got a dog, son."

"I will take care of him. I surely will. You won't *ever* have to feed him, water him, or take him for a walk." That was not, it turned out, the truth, but at the time, it was how I felt.

My dad loved dogs, so Ike became his dog as much as mine. Dad would take Ike for walks after work, maybe to just get some time to himself.

I took Ike to Winston's house after I thought Ike was old enough. Missy didn't even recognize the runt of her litter.

I wanted to write a poem for Katie B, how I felt about her. I didn't know how. That changed when Mrs. Baumgartner had us read a poem called *Winter* by a writer named Blake, William Blake. He lived long ago, in England, but his words seemed to say how I felt about winter. I guess William Blake never played *Annie, Annie Over* in the winter. Our teacher explained the monster in his poem was a metaphor for Winter, with skin and bones.

> *Lo, now the direful monster, whose skin clings*
> *To his strong bones, strides o'er the groaning rocks:*
> *He withers all in silence, and in his hand*
> *Unclothes the earth and freezes up frail life.*

Big words, but she got us understanding.

I was ready to write my poem for Katie B after learning about metaphor. I spent a while at it; finally, I had two lines.

> *A house between us when I caught the ball*
> *thrown over the roof. I wished the ball was you.*

I didn't know how to write more.

I slipped the poem to Katie B when we stood next to each other during a spelling contest. In the cloakroom that day, after recess, we came in last to hang up our coats, put away our boots. She never looked at me after she got my poem. I figured it was a horrible poem, wishing that a tennis ball was her. Katie B looked at me, right in my eyes, kissed me on my cheek, whispered, "I *love* what you wrote to me. I *love* you."

Oh, *Oooooo*, my heart beat so fast. She skipped back to her desk, her skirt swayed like even cloth could be happy.

My life, wintered-in, was no longer frail like William Blake wrote. I was a writer. I could talk to a girl without being near her, my words on paper letting her heart beat like mine, knowing I loved her.

Next week, I had the final two lines for my poem. I could hardly sleep that night, heat lightning throwing shadows of beasts on my bedroom walls. I grabbed the flashlight next to my bed, read again what I wrote for Katie B.

> *And if Missy held you in her mouth all day,*
> *I would never stop chasing her till I got you free.*

I could hardly wait to see her after recess, in the cloak room.

Once you start thinking about your life in poems, how this is like that, such thinking might never end. But Katie B wasn't really a tennis ball. The other thing I needed to know more about was what Mrs. Baumgartner said was the *limp* in a *simile*, which is like a metaphor, but different. I knew what limping meant. A simile was *like* something else, but *not really* the same as something else. Only *like* something else.

I understood better the difference between a simile and real life, between poetry and real life, when snow fell the next week, more snow than ever fell in Dundee.

Snow fell all night.

When I woke, three feet of snow covered our yard and the street in front of our home. Dundee was not ready for that much snow. School got called off. Instead of working on my balsa airplane, I decided I'd write a poem about snow. You couldn't drive a car or truck through the snow in the streets, it was that deep.

Snow seemed like the white lace Aunty Lou crocheted, put on every piece of furniture with a flat top in her home. I had a *simile* I could use.

> *Snow like lace table tops covered our streets,*
> *like on Aunty's tables. Thick, cold lace.*
> *Apple pie would have sunk in it, though,*
> *if you put a hot pie on snow lace.*

Drunk on Love

Winston called me while I worked on my second verse. I never found more to write about snow. Four lines about snow, that was it.

Winston said to get our snow shovel, he'd come by with his shovel, and we'd pick up Chipper, do a good deed.

"What good deed?"

"Will tell you later. Get your snow shovel."

Winston was our leader, so I put on my galoshes, gloves, and wool cap, asked my mom if I could do a good deed with Winston, use our shovel. My mom said that would be fine, just not to get cold in doing our good deed, and be home for lunch.

"You might do a good deed around here, later," mom said. "Shovel snow off our sidewalk, so your dad doesn't hurt his back."

Winston came to our front door wearing a wool cap with flaps over his ears, a snow shovel on his shoulder. We picked up Chipper, headed to our good deed. Ike wanted to come with me, but I had to shut him in. Winston said Mrs. Baumgartner only lived a few blocks away, and she had no one to shovel snow off her driveway and sidewalk.

"Driveway *and* sidewalk?" I said, knowing how long it took to shovel snow off our driveway.

"Right," Winston said.

"A *long* driveway?" Chipper said.

"We'll find out," Winston said. "There's three of us. Doesn't matter how long her driveway might be. My folks said Mrs. Baumgartner could use some help."

We walked past wintry alder trees lining our streets, branches bare of snow, leaves gone, looking like arms of garden scarecrows. Everywhere I looked, *similes*. Poems waiting to be put to paper, not only love poems for Katie B. Thinking about things around me like that did a strange thing to how I felt about my life. I wasn't alone, even when no one was around me. With poems, my life linked up with everything around me, winter, summer, trees, sun, Katie B. Everything was like something else in this world and like me. Even three feet of snow was like me. Mrs. Baumgartner taught me that, about poetry.

I owed her.

It took most of the day to clear snow from her driveway and sidewalk. She gave us hot cocoa with melted marshmallow when we finished, and phoned our folks to tell them she appreciated how they raised us, that we were way better than two clicks above chimps.

High praise, indeed. Later I heard from our Pastor we were a little less than angels. I wondered who was right.

Winston's family left Dundee the next year, but what we learned from him stayed with us. Here's what he taught us: we should be ourselves, have no fear, do what's right, and look out for others. We were on our way to growing up, more than two clicks above chimps.

⁂

Chipper Rhodes lost an arm in the Vietnam War, died of a pain-killer overdose. Chumley West's poor eyesight kept him out of that war; he became a high school basketball coach in California. Minny O'Rourke became a priest, till he married and had a lovely family. T-Bone Zirkel died in a car wreck his senior year in high school. Katie M, my first love, disappeared after she graduated, her body never found. Katie B, my second love, stayed in Dundee, married a dung farmer, and is a gramma now. The sisters with braces never married, became nurses, live somewhere in the Mid-West. Some say they are lesbians. Rowena May joined the SDS movement in college, wanting to end the Vietnam war. She still fights discrimination of any kind.

Dundee looks the same. And maybe it is, kids waiting for another Winston Flats to lead the way to know how to be true to yourself, not harm others. People like Winston don't come along all the time.

After I married Rowena May, when I got out of the service, I became a fly-fishing guide and outdoor sports writer. Rowena May flies my clients in our bush plane. Her brother died in a Vietnamese POW camp, saving another soldier's life in a war that never should have been fought.

We named our oldest son, Winston.

Drunk On Love

What does he remember of love
on an afternoon, drinking her
beauty on grass in woods
after a volcano erupted?

Sun cast shadows on ash
where a blanket was laid,
love songs played.
Space aplenty for minuets,
a waltz, flamenco even—wrapped in heat
from a Prometheus never thanked.

Her, a soft-sift flower dazzling the dead.
Her, so kind, so lovely in her gift. Her, where
curves of this earth are found. Her, who
seemed like the sun, all warmth, fire, and life.

Or so she seemed on an afternoon.

It Happens In Instants

> *Thou, Mastering me,*
> *God!*
>
> Gerard Manley Hopkins, "Wreck of the Deutschland"

Summer, 1965
Night 1. River Rats Float.
Jack Stepovich, Newly Ordained Deacon

I was taught there was a Divine Plan for all of us. The universe was ordered, I was part of that order.

A loud creak from my barn stall's gate; Georgia Rogers. She rode with us in the mayor's raft that day. A sleeping bag under tanned arms, wearing cut-off jeans, and a blouse unbuttoned to her navel. "Sorry to bother you, Jack," her voice nervous, fragile. "Two drunks, cowboys. Can I sleep here, with you? I mean, you know, in your stall, not..."

I nodded, gathered an armful of straw, prepared a space next to me. Outside, the western band wailed, *Smoke, smoke, smoke that cigarette. Puff, puff, puff and if you smoke yourself to death....* I'd thrown my sleeping bag in a horse stall in one of three barns awaiting the River Rats flotilla at Flat Bend, Montana, *The Most Fun Little Town in The West*. Monsignor Hennessey had ordered me to go; an invitation from Mayor Stacy Tillsworth. Georgia unloaded her questions. Did I have a girlfriend? Why not? What's a deacon? Why do I want to be a priest? Do priests have nuns as mistresses? How do I take care of my sexual urges?

I answered her questions as best I could.

"How do you do that?" Georgia said. "No kissing or anything?"

Georgia spotted the two cowboys headed for our stall, grabbed my arm, pressed herself against me, hid her face in the curve of my neck. Her lips, cool against my sunburn.

"It's them, Jack."

I took my open sleeping bag, threw it over her, eased myself and Georgia against the barn wall. Square dance music at the far end of the barn, *Swing your lady from Arkansas, strut your stuff in front of her pa...* Georgia kissed my neck. In becoming a deacon, I promised to live celibate. Unsure what to do, I froze. Georgia sighed, nibbled my ear.

"If you do that again, Georgia, I'll have to throw off this sleeping bag. Those cowboys will see you. You're a lovely girl but..."

"Girl? A *girl*? I'm a woman," Georgia said. "Don't I look like a woman? I think you're handsome and not like other guys who just want a feel or a roll in the hay."

"My life, now, doesn't include girls," I said. "I mean women. You're very attractive, but..."

She silenced me, a finger on my lips. "Ministers marry and God doesn't care. They kiss their wives before they get married. What's God got to do with a kiss?"

"I'm not going to be a minister. God wants celibacy for priests, so he frowns on priests kissing."

"For shame."

"*What*?"

"For shame. Your Church thinks God respects priests more than ministers."

"I don't know who God respects more. My Church says deacons and priests can't marry and that includes kissing, now or later."

"Oooo, sweet. Say that again, *now or later*. I love how you look. So serious."

"Don't you have serious goals you'll sacrifice for?"

"Is that what we're doing?" she said. "I mean, *you* sacrifice and if *you* sacrifice, *I* have to sacrifice? Everybody sacrificing, and I just want to kiss you, so I'd know what you kissed like and wouldn't wake up regretting I didn't kiss this man who is so handsome and so serious."

"I'm not handsome. And I'm not always..."

"When are you not serious? All day you've been serious, like waiting for a bank to open. Ever watch folks wait for a bank to open? They're serious. Even if they smile, they look serious. That's you, smiling." She studied me. I saw a new Georgia, aware, alert, nobody's fool.

I grew silent, thought over what she said. "If I kiss you, does that mean I know how not to be serious?"

"It might." She moved close.

"Awww, *kiss her, Jack*," the cowboy said, leaning on the stall gate, wiping dust from the Stetson in his hand. Hair tassels sprouted from his head like corn cob strands. He had a gaunt leather face, swayed to music or liquor; I couldn't tell which. A shorter cowboy with a walleye tipped his hat. Two of my future faithful?

"I don't believe we've met, fellows. I'm Jack Stepovich."

"He's a gentleman, Freddy!" the tall cowboy said. "Didya hear that; *I don't believe we've met?* And he don't kiss girls. That's some kind of gentleman. Pardner, I call ever-body *Jack*. Jeezus, his name is Jack. What you think about that, Freddy?"

"That's a good 'un," the Cyclops said, snorted his nose clean.

"We're having a private conversation. Would you mind leaving us alone?" I tried not to sound challenging.

"Freddy and me don't have nowheres to sleep, friend Jack, an' thought y'all might like company. Seeing how there's plenty of the little lady to go around, and you don't want any of her."

The corn-head wiped spit from his lips, winked at Georgia. She threw aside my sleeping bag, jumped to her feet. "Get out of here if you don't want jail time," Georgia said. "My dad's sheriff here and one word, one word from me and he'll lock you up. So Fuck *OFF*."

I tried not to look at her jean-wrapped derriere. Noise from the band and cracks of thunder outside did not dull the confidence of Georgia's threat.

"Hey, sweetheart, no big deal," the tall cowboy said, put on his Stetson. "You don't want hard candy tonight, so we'll mosey on." They left.

George sat down. "Sorry I involved you, Jack."

"I didn't help much. Your dad is…?"

"No. Just made that up." Georgia put an arm on an upraised knee, nestled her chin on her arm. "Would you have fought to preserve my honor?"

I relaxed, leaned against the stall wall. "My mom would disown me if I didn't. I grew up on a farm. She taught my brother and me to protect women from men like them."

"I like your mom. But, not much honor to save. I stopped being a virgin three years ago when I was sixteen. Gone to bed with a dozen guys. I'm tired of it. Like a Halloween pumpkin who's gone to all the celebrations; Christmas, Easter, Fourth of July," she said, "and can't remember what was meant to be special for me."

"I was to be another on the list?"

"Don't put it like that, please." Georgia looked down.

"Sorry. I didn't mean that."

I opened my arms. She moved snugly against me, asked if we could sleep with our arms around each other. We settled back to watch the dancing, hopping, yelling and condensation of sweat on the faces of River Rats floaters I would serve as a priest next year when I turned twenty-six.

I looked at Georgia, asleep beside me, wanted to wake her, explain why I couldn't accept her offer. Not only because I was a priest-to-be, but she didn't offer the quality of the gift I'd received the previous summer. I refused Georgia not only because of a commitment to celibacy but because of a desire I could not escape, growing in me since reading the poetry of Gerard Manley Hopkins. I'd begun a quest I didn't understand. Here's what I began: I wanted to know, yearned to know, to experience, *God*. If God existed, why wait till death to seek union with the Divine?

I recalled the summer before I was ordained a deacon when I experienced the most unexpected union with the Mystery. I met her on a train. In Italy.

I hitchhiked south from Holland, rode trains when I reached Italy to speed up the trip, so I could have time with my family at home before fall classes on the East Coast. I shared a compartment on the train between Pisa and Florence with a woman my age, so stunning, so lovely, she seemed like a Botticelli painting, ethereal, emerging from an eternally white clamshell. She sat modestly on her side of the compartment across from me, erect, her hands holding a book on her lap, the title, in French—*Les Fleurs du mal*. Flowers of Evil. I had never heard of it. More sophisticated than any woman I'd ever met. She wore a white blouse fringed tight at her neck, grey skirt to just below her knees, hair tinted lightly red, in a ponytail. I wore a sports jacket I bought for ten dollars from a seminarian who hitched through Europe the summer before. Dirty shirts, slacks, socks, and day-old cheese filled my backpack. I wanted to discover if I should remain at St. Luke's Seminary, become a parish priest—or leave to become a monk. I spent time each summer at a Trappist monastery in Utah.

We listened silently to the *slickity-slack* of the train on the tracks. She looked up, caught me studying her, smiled. *Bonjour*, she said gently. My tongue stuck. She widened her eyes, tried to help me speak.

B-b-bonjour, I finally said, using the French I learned in the seminary. We relaxed, had a language to share. She told me she was returning from the Sorbonne, majoring in French literature. I forgot I was anything other than a man at that moment. I wasn't a seminarian, studying to become a priest. Nothing seemed important to me except her.

Love. What else to call the feeling? I felt dizzy. She was an overwhelming presence. Was I naïve? Probably, but I had never felt anything like it before. *So, this is how it feels, to experience the Mystery, without any barrier? Matter and Spirit, as one, no difference.*

At one point she asked if I had any favorite wisdom from French literature. I laughed, told her I only knew *L'enfer, c'est les autres.* Sartre. Hell is other people.

She smiled.

"Perhaps, someday, try Baudelaire? She closed her eyes, spoke to me in a melodious voice words I only later understood: *"Il faut être toujour ivre..."*

Be drunk! So as not to be the martyred slaves of time, be drunk, be continually drunk! On wine, on poetry or on virtue, as you wish.

When the train stopped at Empoli, we said our good-byes, got off to change trains, her to go south to Siena. I would catch the train to Florence, see the *Duomo*, take a train south to Rome. At the train station, I had discovered I left my camera in its leather case hanging on a hook next to the window in the compartment, but the train had left. I rushed to her, told her, *J'ai perdu mon camera.* She hurried with me to tell the Stationmaster. The Stationmaster would call ahead to Florence, he said, have them look for my *amico.*

"You think I lost my friend?" I said. "You think I lost my friend on the train?"

"*Oui,*" she said. "You said, *J'ai perdu mon comarade; your amico.*"

I mimed a camera in my hands, snapped photos. The Stationmaster said he'd call ahead for my *macchina fotografica.* To thank her, I bought her a warm coke from a machine, sat with her at an outdoor station table until her train arrived. She asked if I might come through Siena on my way to Rome, spend time with her at her parents' villa. I wanted to, more than I wanted anything in my life at that moment. Her train began to pull away. She jumped up, ran for the train, I ran beside her. She could run like a deer, ponytail swaying wildly. She shouted a question.

"*Viens-tu?*" Will you come see me?

"*Peut-être*" I yelled, running next to her. Perhaps. (Of course, I couldn't.)

She stopped, scribbled a phone number on a yellow train ticket stub, placed it in my hand, looked in my eyes, jumped aboard the caboose.

"*Au revoir*," I yelled. I thought I said good-bye,

"*Au revoir?*" she called to me, confused. *Until I see you* is what I said.

She stood quietly, her eyes never leaving mine until she could no longer see me. She blew me a kiss as her train curved out of sight.

You must understand, this was 1964—everything we knew about Truth was changing.

Siena, Italy

Nicola took my hand, lead me outside her family's home to the orchard behind a low rock wall. We came to the caretaker's stone cottage. The afternoon haze over the city moved toward the villa. A rooster crowed from a perch next to the cottage.

"Paolo is in town, Jacques. A holiday for him and his family. He left us wine."

She tucked the loose white blouse tightly in her jeans, standing much shorter than me even in her heeled sandals. I loved how she said my name, *Jacques*. It made me seem not-me, someone else. "My special place," she said. "I wanted to be here, with you, before you left. I lived my fantasies here as a girl. I am open to these rooms as I am to you. Like the first time I came here, I was open to you before we spoke on the train. I might not always have this little house. I can't always have you, but for now I have you both. Do you understand?"

"I have special places, Nicola. I'll enjoy yours," I said, relaxed.

After closing window curtains, she poured us wine, told about her memories in the cottage as a girl before her father hired a caretaker.

"Cheer?" She tried to speak English, clinked her glass to mine.

"*Cheers*. I should tell you more about myself, Nicola. Later you might..."

"No, I only ask this, Jacques," she interrupted. "Do you have a girlfriend? Are you married?"

"I have no girlfriend, am not married. That's what you thought I wanted to tell you? My hesitation in coming to see you?"

"Yes."

"That's not a concern. I must leave tomorrow; it's not likely I will see you again."

"It's not likely we would have even met. Do you believe in Kismet? I do."

I told her I knew only a little about Kismet. She explained her belief in fated love connections. *Not a Plan. Fate.* I flashed ahead. Next year, the diaconate, celibacy, God's Plan for my life.

"Jacques, you want me?"

Perspiration formed along my temples, beneath my arms, dryness came to my throat. Staring at me, she moved a hand to her blouse, undid the top button. I bent down, placed my lips to her offered neck. Standing upright, silhouetted against the curtained windows showering us with sunlight, we nudged buttons holding our clothes. My desire, since reading the poetry of Gerard Manley Hopkins, was to experience Divine Incarnate Mystery in the fleeting world around me.

Don't flee when It comes.

Nicola eased my shirt to the floor, undid my watch, placed it on the table. I wanted to run. She slid her hands over my chest, fingers through my hair; more blond due to summer sun. She kissed my collarbone. In my ear she whispered, *Kismet.*

I copied her actions, my hands becoming sure, cupping her breasts beneath her gaze. Knowing her with my hands brought me closer to the fusion I sought of spiritual awareness and the materiality of myself. She looked up, puzzled. Facial muscles that pulled her eyes together gave way to a smile. Her eyes traced my nose, lips, chin, came to rest on my neck. She lightly kissed my neck. The puzzled look worked its way again to her face. I couldn't move, couldn't respond to her softness wrapped in jeans.

"No, Jacques? You don't want to become drunken with me, drinking me all you want?"

I told her, embarrassed, *Je ne sais pa...comment.* I didn't know...how to make love.

"Oh." She studied me, nestled closer in my arms, danced slowly with me over the stone floor. "I understand, *caro mio.* I had a first time, too." She smiled, hummed against my chest, traced with her hands the farm-carved muscles of my back as if she was a student of Michelangelo's *Torso* and knew the terrain by heart.

"I want to make love with you, Jacques. Now. I don't care if you leave tomorrow."

The belt around her waist fell from her hand to the stone floor. I undid the button at her waist, kissed her between the cypress of her neck and willow of her waist. On my knees, I waited for her to walk to me, hold my head with her hands. I tried to remove her jeans. She moved to place her weight on one foot, arched toward the ceiling, eased the jeans down her thighs. She stepped out of the jeans so gracefully they remained in place on the floor.

She sucked blood beneath my ribs to the surface of skin, helped me remove my jeans, knelt to survey my body, removed my shorts. Glancing upward, she caught me in a moment of curiosity. Nicola smiled, stood to embrace me, her silky body letting me know what I would miss if I never returned to her.

※

Now I knew, loving a woman; overwhelming.

Would becoming one with the Mystery mean more? Yes, of course.

※

Day 2. River Rats Float.

"So, you're becoming a preacher?" the *National Geographic* photographer said, prying open a beer in the mayor's raft on our float downriver.

Contemptuous? *Preacher* evoked tent meetings, Elmer Gantry. Maybe not. Did much of anything float in the head of the man who looked at life through a Nikon lens?

"You could say that," I told him.

"Bill," the woman from *National Geographic* said. "Jack will become a priest, not a preacher. You know better."

So, a sarcastic remark. Jill Austin-Cooper, the photographer's companion, would know.

Mayor Tillsworth invited interesting companions to share his rubber raft for the three-day journey. Besides me, the mayor invited a woman who wrote for the *National Geographic* to tell America about his community event, bring tourist dollars west. Jill Austin-Copper brought with her a photographer, Bill, the man who resented me. The mayor also invited Georgia Rogers, who sold clothes to his wife at Yarding's Department Store.

After we passed under a bridge, Georgia kicked off her sandals, removed her blouse and shorts to suntan in the swimsuit she wore underneath. Sheer black lace connected a tiny black top with a petite bottom. Georgia's copper-toned limbs rested crucified next to me.

The reporter, Jill Austin-Copper, broke the silence, summarized the swimsuit, "That's a clever use of cow ears, dear." Jill had prematurely grey hair, worn in a short soup-bowl cut.

Georgia smiled, placed her shapely, tanned legs on the beer cooler in front of her.

"Angus ears, ma'am. The only thing not black-as-coal on an Angus heifer is her big white udders. Course, from the East, you mightn't know much about big udders."

Georgia made sure all was in place under her bikini top, laid back on the raft rim, put on sunglasses. I admired her cool. Jill flitted her eyebrows at Georgia, in disgust; the younger woman easily winning the feminine joust. Bill couldn't keep his eyes off Georgia.

"Jack, did you get your night prayers said last night with Georgia in your stall and all the yelling and dancing?" Bill said. Why wouldn't he shut-the-hell up, stop taunting me?

"I asked Jack to protect me from drunks," Georgia said. "That's all."

"Didn't mean to imply anything. How about a shot of you and Jack sharing a paddle, sweetheart? I'll use a wide-angle lens and get the rest of those boats in the background."

"Later," Georgia said, irritated.

Georgia stretched out in the rear of the raft, let her right arm dangle in the cold water. Her left arm rested along the ridge of the raft, behind the paddles and life jackets piled between us. Her fingers gently rubbing my arm.

By sun-straight-up, the photographer was drunk, hurled empty beer cans at passing boats. "Now, I got to pee. Tell me, Jack. Do priests hold their *thing* when they pee, or is there some special clerical way to make water?"

"We don't pee, Bill. Just one of those things about the priestly life," I said. "Tell me, do photographers do anything worth photographing?" I didn't have to take his crap.

Georgia guffawed.

"If you don't pee, then you never have any reason to hold it at all, Jack. Bet you wonder what that thing between your legs is for."

"I find it less troublesome than wondering what the thing between my ears is for."

"Seems a waste," Bill said. "Balls on a priest. Nothing personal, Jack, I mean, take that pretty thing next to you. Nobody would know or care if you two, you know. I wouldn't. I'm not decadent. Got a wife and two kids and a dog named Spot. Oh, well, not my concern. I got to pee. Sorry folks. Bill Boy is so full of pee, his ribs float."

L'enfer, c'est les autres—especially a moron named Bill.

The photographer stood, faced to the starboard side while we floated downstream. He waved at boats, fumbled with his zipper. Mayor Tillsworth yelled to sit down.

Shouts from a boat behind us. I shot upright. The concrete foundation of a bridge loomed ahead. I yelled for Bill to sit down. Our raft rammed the concrete head-on, Bill catapulted head-first against the concrete into water. The impact flung Georgia off the raft. For a moment, both Bill and Georgia bobbed into view. The photographer floated unconscious, Georgia flayed wildly. Rapids ahead. Impossible to save both. Boats revved up engines to reach Bill and Georgia.

"Help him!" Jill screamed.

Bill's body rolled, disappeared.

I dove in, came up, both bodies in front of me.

The Float Marshal wrapped a blanket around me, offered a cup of hot coffee. "You did just fine, son."

I accepted the coffee, looked at the body wrapped in a blanket on grass next to me. Georgia coughed, rolled over. Jill sat hunched against a log near the fire, sobbing. She glanced up, anger in her eyes.

Jill whispered, "How can I explain this to Bill's wife? I've been having an affair with him, and she knows it. She'll blame me; I begged him to come on this trip."

"His drowning was an accident," I told her.

"Tell that to his wife and kids."

I put down the coffee cup, walked to the edge of the river, watched the search for Bill's body. I didn't hear the footsteps behind me until I heard her voice.

"It could be Bill wrapped alive in that blanket. You made the decision, you fucking-fake. You must live with it. *Why*? Why save her? You slept with her? He was a great artist, a good father."

"I wanted to save both. I couldn't. And I didn't *sleep* with her."

"Is that what they teach you? Save the sex kitten, let the drunk drown? You never tried to save him, and you know it. Both were there, in front of you. You grabbed for the girl and let Bill drown."

"I'm sorry. I'll call his family."

"Like hell you will."

※

Monsignor Hennessey banged the phone in its cradle, stomped back to the rectory dining room where Father Sean O'Reilly and I had dinner with the monsignor. This, the third reporter's inquiry concerning the deacon who saved the woman but had not, according to another witness, done all he could to save the man.

"Ya put me in a bind, Jack. The bishop called to find out what happened and what I might be doing about it." He sliced his steak, stabbed it with a fork, angry.

"I told you what happened. I couldn't save both. She came to get away from drunks and that's all that happened between us."

"Here's what they ask, 'Is it true Reverend Mr. Jack Stepovich resides at St. Mary's rectory? I'd like to confirm he spent the night alone in a horse stall with the young woman he rescued.'"

Sean O'Reilly, assistant pastor of St. Mary's, kept his attention riveted on his plate.

"O, Man," Monsignor Hennessey said, "if a juicy Colleen knocks on my horse stall complaining the boys are trying to have a shady score, do I let her sleep in my stall? I hear this girl was attractive."

"What do her looks have to do with it?" Irish religiosity—it didn't belong in America.

"Ah, Man, ya know what her looks got to do with it. Never knew ya, as a boy, Jack, to play stupid. What they teach you lads in the seminary? I've said this often, right, Sean? Young people today forget the old rules. Priests do not, I repeat, sir, do not sleep in horse stalls with women. Especially pretty colleens. Especially with the place jammers and folks dancing and watching. You did not answer me. Was she attractive?" He put down his fork, waited my response.

"You're getting into internal forum questions," I told him, prepared to duel it out.

"Internal forum, *my arse*! I didn't ask you if you committed sin with her. I presume you committed no sin. I asked a simple question, was she attractive?"

"Yes."

"Did she make a pass at you?"

"I shouldn't be revealing her life at this table."

"So, she did," the Monsignor said. "I must know the truth. An accident, and you should get a medal on your chest for risking your life, but the press smells another story, and they've got that Jill woman giving it." He folded his hands across his huge chest, ready to be my judge and jury.

"I would let her sleep in my stall again if the circumstances were the same."

"Did you kiss? I got a right to that information as your superior not as your confessor."

I looked him in his now-alert blue eyes. "She kissed me, a kiss that didn't mean a thing to me."

Monsignor Hennessey banged the table, stared at the dining room chandelier.

"Holy Mother of God! You spend hours in the church, meditating! You should be with parishioners. Now you tell me a sexy dame kissed you in a horse stall, and it didn't mean a thing. O, Man, kissing means something. Right, Sean? Kissing that girl means a horse's arse was in that stall. What staying in that stall would look like. I asked the bishop to transfer you to St. Raphael's, across town, for the rest of the summer, son. You speak Spanish well enough, so you can communicate with all those Mexican beet pickers. I can't have the people of this parish buzzin' about this."

"When do you want me to leave?" I wanted OUT of this straight-jacket rectory.

"Father Stanley will make your acquaintance tomorrow, Reverend Mister Jack."

For the remainder of the summer I lived at St. Raphael's, practiced my sermons in Spanish, visited migrant workers at Holy Cross Hospital, organized a Little League baseball team for the boys of the parish, carried Communion to those too sick to get to church.

Saturday evenings I had supper with Georgia at her apartment, discreetly, after she finished work at Yarding's Department store. Although I had less time for meditation, I complied with Monsignor Hennessey's words to spend more time with parishioners, less time meditating and seeking union with the Mystery.

We cooked together, did the dishes, played cribbage until ten o'clock. She never accepted dates Saturday night, never touched me or hinted we should become involved. She came to know my past, my beliefs about God.

Our last evening, after dishes, Georgia said, "I never thought I could fall in love with a man except in the physical way. Now I know I can." She kissed my cheek. "Thanks, Jack, for everything."

I boarded the train for my final year at St. Luke's Seminary, that summer, '65. Sitting in my compartment, I realized the only time I wasn't overcome by feeling alone, or lonely, was with Georgia, but even she barely touched the periphery of my separateness. The train rolled and tossed, *slickity-slack*, reminding me of the train ride from Pisa, of Nicola.

Is that as close as Matter and Spirit get?

It happens in instants. Like in Siena.

Then—*Poof*, gone.

Father Jack Stepovich, 1966

Monsignor Hennessey walked beside me to the altar in the church where I'd served as his altar boy. I had a troubling realization. I never learned how to offer a High Mass. My grandparents thought I spent eight years in the seminary learning how to say Mass. Only the briefest part of my diaconate year concerned learning anything liturgical. While the monsignor pointed to the proper prayers, whispered directions, I bumbled into a truth about myself. I didn't care much about liturgical acts, incense, hosts or blessing people.

How could I spend eight years preparing for this day and not know?

As a boy, a peace grew in me, gazing across prairie, watching storms heave and roll. The peace came from a sense of having nothing important to do, not the calm after a deed of some magnitude.

A poster Monsignor Hennessey tacked up in the church foyer during National Vocation Week trumpeted my first divine Call. Three boys dressed in black suits, white shirts, and black ties, walked like Knights of the Round Table down a path in front of a monastic building. The poster announced God sought young men willing to give their lives for the salvation of others.

I was fourteen.

That first Divine trumpet-blast petered out somewhere in my inner ear canal. My life at the time was about me, not about saving anyone else.

The second blast came when I read poetry for a term paper my junior year in high school. I selected Gerard Manley Hopkins' poem, *The Wreck of the Deutschland*, for an exegesis, contrary to the wishes of my teacher who studied only Byron, Shelley, Keats, Whitman and Frost.

I am soft sift, wrote Hopkins. *In an hourglass, at the wall Fast, but mined with a motion, a drift, and it crowds, and it combs to the fall.*

The words were not a Marine Corps summons to serve Uncle Sam or a call to frolic with God to save souls.

The words were about; what?

About Mystery.

I found a volume of Hopkins' poetry and read aloud to the Montana moor and dappled sky of *couple-color*, the half-finished rushes of Hopkins' yearning for the Center of Things. These weren't sermons laced with sleeping pills that put my father and me to sleep. An omnipotent Presence charged into the world, glimpsed through *brindled cows, groins of the braes*, and the shook foil of God's presence, reflected everywhere. And words that overpowered me—

Thou mastering me
God.

To save the world seemed a foolish quest since, on the prairie, the land didn't seem in need of saving as much as watering, plowing, and leaving alone to cycles of growth and decay and rejuvenation. Where except a seminary could Hopkins' awareness of God's mysterious presence be pursued in America?

The seminary jostled my interest in union with God, directed me to rituals, to the God-Man Jesus Christ, to Sin. The idea of *Church* began to make more sense as *Sin* became more real. My God-yearnings receded as the ecclesiastical Shadow enlarged in my awareness. I was on the brink of great revelations that never came, on the brink of what Hopkins wrote about. I would give myself to others, as the poster of my youth urged, hoped spiritual union with Mystery, with God, might visit me in ministering to others.

When my ordination Mass ended, I went to the communion rail, blessed people kneeling there. They kissed my hands, my mother wept, so did my father. The bishop assigned me to serve as assistant pastor in another parish, far from my home town. I'd made a promise to myself when I lay prostrate at my ordination. I would never allow the sun to set without reminding myself the Godhead is Unknowable, yet, God is a Mystery present in the world around me, as Hopkins wrote.

How to stay attuned with the Mystery while performing the exhausting duties of a parish priest?

I settled on a simple solution. Whenever I met someone, I'd say silently to myself, "I love you," remind myself the Mystery filling the universe also flowed in all others.

A woman phoned, identified herself as Bonnet Elk Horn, an Indian from the reservation a half-day's bus ride from town. Bonnet had a problem. She wished to return to the Church. Would I drive downtown to the pay phone, pick up her and her son, hear her confession at the rectory?

The young boy said nothing when I lifted him from his stroller, handed him to his mother in the car. "I love you," I said silently to the boy.

Bonnet hadn't been to church for years, wished to confess, become reinstated with the Church. Sitting in the living room of the rectory, she made her confession. Afterward she revealed the real reason for her visit. Her husband would be released from the state penitentiary in a week. She had to get rid of the man she had lived with the past year of her husband's confinement at Deer Lodge penitentiary.

"I love you," I repeated silently to the child on Bonnet's knee, and to her. Having made this bond with another fragment of divinity, I couldn't abandon her, even after suspecting I'd been duped.

"He might beat me, Father, and hurt my child, his son. I promised him I would remain..."

I crossed my legs beneath my cassock, folded the purple stole I took from around my neck, dropped the stole on the rug.

"What can I do for you, Mrs. Elk Horn?" I asked as quietly as she spoke to me. I didn't know how long the Crow had lived in Montana, or anything about their customs.

"Come to our place, Father. Tell this man I must leave him before my husband comes back, so I can stay in the Church." She glanced at me but was more intent on the quiet boy toying with the cross she wore around her neck. *The boy was part of the Plan for her, or part of her Kismet?*

"Tell the man you live with that you have to leave him, so you can stay in the Church?"

"I have no other way, Father. My only chance to stay safe and keep my baby safe. And, Father, I love my husband. I had no money, nowhere to go. You understand?"

"I will come, Mrs. Elk Horn. But I can't come today since I have a meeting. Tomorrow?"

"What time?"

"One o'clock? Will he be home?"

"Yes, Father. I will tell him a priest comes. He's not Catholic. I am happy, Father, so very happy you come. My son means everything to me." She hugged her son, tears in her eyes.

When meeting the man, I said to myself, "I love you," to the Mystery in him, walked into their apartment. He stood taller than me, wore jeans, a plaid shirt neatly tucked into a beaded belt, long hair down to his shoulders. After explaining why I came, the man got up without a word, and left the room.

Bonnet followed him, returned. "He told me to tell you to leave, Father. He says I'm his woman no matter what the priest says." She waited for a message to carry back to the bedroom. I copied Calvary-Indian movies I watched when a boy, fingered the tight roman collar I wore for confidence that I had the right, the obligation, to intervene in her life. Be part of the Plan for her.

"Tell him you will go to hell if you die in sin. He won't want you to go to hell, will he?"

"I don't know, Father. I will tell him."

She returned, hands clasped in front of her, tears in her eyes. Her son ran into the room.

"If you don't leave, he will throw you out, Father. That's what he says. He's very strong."

The man stormed into the living room, waving a revolver. He hit Bonnet, knocked her down. The gun fired, pain stabbed my shoulder. Bonnet jumped up, grabbed the gun as the man fired again.

The bullet ripped into his head. I didn't know his name. I held her son, tried to comfort him, while she phoned the police.

Our Lady of Mercy Monastery
Father Paul, 1979

I had my Trappist monk name, a new identity at the Utah monastery. I'd gone again to my confessor, the Abbot, for spiritual guidance. Thirteen years since I became a parish priest, but now a monk, seeking union with the Mystery, nothing diverting my attention. No parish duties.

"The Dark Night of the Soul, Father Paul. It comes to all of us who seek Him alone. Our Lord's deepest embrace. Be patient," the Abbot said. He always looked me in the eye when counseling me. He'd grown up in Chicago. I wanted to believe him.

I'd enjoyed the solitude of monastic life for five years after the man's death, a day's end at nine o'clock, sleeping on a straw-filled mattress. I loved chanting in chapel after waking at three-thirty in the morning, working in the wheat fields that strengthened the muscles of my youth, work done in silence, sign language between us while we drove tractors, lived a farmhand's life. These years of monastic living became the quiet joyousness of living the Plan for my life. Seeking union with the Mystery called God.

A year earlier I recognized only the routine of my life buoyed me up, made it possible to live with neurotic G.I.s who fled to monasteries following two wars. My reason for being there faded. I was losing my faith, *God* only a word. I pursued the Mystery behind the word only to have it closed, spirited away

Drunk on Love

to a black hole somewhere in the universe. In the chapel, my chanting seemed directed to a void. No divine arm stretched out to bring me home. I prayed to Nothingness.

What became clear to me, there is no God.

"For how long, Reverend Father?" I said. "Over a year since I believed. I'm a fake, as someone once told me. I pray, but don't believe Anyone listens. I'm not going through the Dark Night of the Soul, like you say. I lost my faith. I don't believe I do any good with my prayers."

My head, shaved except for the close-cropped tonsure-ring of hair, gone the golden locks my mother took pride in when I was a child. Not even my mother could visit me, except twice a year in the Guest House. My father no longer came to see me.

The Abbot handed me a bundle of letters.

"From your family and friends. Get more sleep, Father Paul. Let God find you."

One of the letters contained a news story. The headlines read, "WOMAN STRANGLED." Smaller type said, "Husband Confesses." The clipping came from the town newspaper where I worked my first two years as a priest, sent to me by my mother.

> *The body of a Native woman was found behind the Missouri Bar last night by police officers who had been directed to the spot by the woman's estranged husband. The victim, Bonnet Elk Horn, had been strangled with a belt. The victim's husband, George Elk Horn, confessed the alleged murder to the authorities several hours after the incident. He is being held without bail pending an investigation.*

A follow-up story was attached.

> *Sister Mercedez, a social worker from St. Mary's Convent, explained that the brutal murder of Bonnet Elk Horn in March of this year by her husband must be put in a proper framework to understand the tragedy. "Mr. Elk Horn has not been himself since his release from prison seven years ago," the nun told reporters. "He couldn't get work because of his prison record. His wife washed dishes at the Bar to support the family." The Catholic nun added, "It was degrading for him to not be able to support his wife and child. In his hatred for himself, under the influence*

of alcohol, he took her life so she would not see him in his humiliated state. The system killed Bonnet, not her husband. He loved her enough to kill her," the nun said. *The District Attorney warned the press not to be "lulled into fainthearted nunishness by the good Sister, who means well but who can't see the obvious fact that we have a murderer among us."*

I broke my vow of obedience, fled the refectory to the fading daylight. I climbed the treeless hill behind the monastery, tripped on my robes but got to my feet, climbed higher. Vespers bells below. I lay on rocky ground, watched stars fleck the black Utah sky.

"That's it," I said, wiping tears. "You say nothing, so I say nothing to You. I live alone. You're not there. If You were there, I'd not be needed so Bonnet's son had a mom. But if You're not there with the Bonnets of the world, *why the hell should I be?*"

Bonnet's son took his time warming to me, my shaved head only beginning to sprout hair again. He knew I tried to protect his mother. "Maybe," was all he'd say. He'd think about living with me a few weeks each summer, on our farm, with a couple of his close cousins. I'd teach him what I knew about riding horses, roping calves, milking cows, playing baseball against the barn backstop, swimming in waterholes.

"Okay, if I can visit my dad," he finally said. I promised him we'd see his father at Deer Lodge Penitentiary whenever he wished to go. And not miss the summer Crow Pow-Wow.

I neatly folded my leather jacket, placed it in the overhead bin, settled in for a long flight. I felt lighter than air. I'd lost the core of my identity up till then: becoming one with the Mystery. I tried to recall *Jack,* as a boy experiencing the world as it was, not concealed in religious fantasy.

The yellow train ticket stub had her phone number. She had a daughter, she said, and was divorced. "Intoxicating wine awaits you, Jacques. *Chianti Vecchio*—a finely aged Tuscany, like me. Hurry, hurry, *tempus fugit,* caro mio."

Acknowledgments

"The Phaedra" received an award for anthropological fiction from the Society for Anthropology and Humanism and was published in the *Anthropology and Humanism Quarterly,* 14(4):132-134.

"Take My Yacht, Please" appeared in *Cirque: A Literary Journal for the North Pacific Rim,* Summer 2017, Vol. 8, No. 2.

"It Happens In Instants" derives from a novel in progress.

About the Author

Kerry Dean Feldman grew up on *The Badlands* of Montana, taught to read and write at age five by his mother—Kathyrn "Peaches" Hauk. She could break horses and play basketball in her teens, loved literature.

He co-originated with Jack Lobdell (1974) the still vibrant Alaska Anthropological Association. He is Professor Emeritus of Anthropology at the University of Alaska Anchorage.

Franny and Zooey, in his teens, changed his notions of fiction-truth, helped him discover the Western canon—still inspired by Aristophanes' socially critical (and humorous) drama, Chaucer's mind-boggling *Canterbury Tales,* the illusions of Cervantes' *Don Quixote.* He studied the languages and literatures of the Romans, Greeks, Spanish, French, Hebrew—to peer deeper into how Western reality formed him, both to appreciate and critique.

To him, there are many ways to be human, and to love.

He sees romantic love as a rodeo (he's from Montana, after all), culturally given, historically grounded. You ride an exquisite Wildness, the Wild gores you, maybe you take the loving Wild home,

AND,

the real rodeo begins.

About the Artist

Tami Phelps is a mixed-media artist using cold wax medium, assemblage, and fine art photography, who lives and works in Anchorage, Alaska. Her hand-colored photography and cold wax medium art are in the permanent collections of the Anchorage Museum at Rasmuson Center, and Museum of Encaustic Art (MoEA) in Santa Fe, NM. Tami is the sole artist from Alaska selected for the MoEA Exhibition: "50 States, 200 Artists" (July 2019).

Her work provokes thought, each piece evolving in its own direction. Her work has exhibited in Alaska, Colorado, New Mexico, and Washington. Cirque Journal featured her work on the cover of their summer solstice issue, 2017.

She enjoys travel to expand her skills in making art and photographic images, most recently a workshop in Drezzo, Italy with her cold wax idols, Rebecca Crowell and Jerry McLaughlin. She might attach unique vintage objects, metal, and fabric to help interpret her art and tell its story.

The cover photograph, *Anniversary Rose After 33 Years*, draws on her exhibit, "HER STORIES," at the International Gallery of Contemporary Art in Anchorage, Alaska (May 2018).

Her art often reflects her love of laughter, sometimes through tears.

About Cirque Press

Cirque Press grew out of *Cirque*, a literary journal established in 2009 by Michael Burwell, as a vehicle for the publication of writers and artists of the North Pacific Rim. This region is broadly defined as reaching north from Oregon to the Yukon Territory and south through Alaska to Hawaii – and east to the Russian Peninsula. Sandra Kleven joined *Cirque* in 2012 working as a partner with Burwell.

Our contributors are widely published in an array of journals. Their writing is significant. It is personal. It is strong. It draws on these regions in ways that add to the culture of places.

We felt that the works of individual writers could be lost if they were to remain scattered across the literary landscape. Therefore, we established a press to collect these writing efforts. Cirque Press (2017) seeks to gather the work of our contributors into book-form where it can be experienced coherently as statement, observation, and artistry.

Sandra Kleven – Michael Burwell, publishers and editors
cirquepressaknw@gmail.com
www.cirquejournal.com

Books from Cirque Press

Apportioning the Light by Karen Tschannen (2018)
The Lure of Impermanence by Carey Taylor (2018)
Echolocation by Kristin Berger (2018)
Like Painted Kites & Collected Works by Clifton Bates (2019)
Athabascan Fractal: Poems of the Far North by Karla Linn Merrifield (2019)
Holy Ghost Town by Tim Sherry (2019)
Drunk on Love: Twelve Stories to Savor Responsibly by Kerry Dean Feldman (2019)
Seward Soundboard by Sean Ulman (2019)
Silty Water People by Vivian Faith Prescott (2019)

Made in the USA
Columbia, SC
21 May 2020